The *Mountain*
of adventure

Enid Blyton, who died in 1968, is one of the most successful children's authors of all time. She wrote over seven hundred books, which have been translated into more than forty languages and have sold more than 400 million copies around the world. Enid Blyton's stories of magic, adventure and friendship continue to enchant children the world over. Enid Blyton's beloved works include The Famous Five, Malory Towers, The Faraway Tree and the Adventure series.

Titles in the Adventure series:

The *Mountain*

of adventure

Enid Blyton

MACMILLAN CHILDREN'S BOOKS

First published 1949 by Macmillan Children's Books

This edition published 2007 by Macmillan Children's Books
a division of Macmillan Publishers Limited
20 New Wharf Road, London N1 9RR
Associated companies throughout the world
www.panmacmillan.com

ISBN 978-0-330-44837-6

13 15 17 19 18 16 14

A CIP catalogue record for this book is available from
the British Library.

Typeset by Intype Libra Ltd
Printed and bound in the UK by CPI Group (UK) Ltd, Croydon, CR0 4YY

Contents

1

All set for a summer holiday

Four children were singing at the tops of their voices in a car that was going up a steep mountain-side road.

A parrot was also joining in, very much out of tune, cocking up her crest in excitement. The man at the wheel turned round with a grin.

'I say! I can't even hear the car hooter. What's the matter with you all?'

Philip, Jack, Dinah and Lucy-Ann stopped singing and shouted answers at him.

'It's the beginning of the hols!'

'And we're going to have a donkey each to ride in the mountains!'

'Pop goes the weasel!' That was Kiki the parrot, of course, joining in.

'We've got eight weeks of fun all together.'

'And you'll be with us, Bill, as well as Mother! Mother, aren't you excited too?'

Mrs Mannering smiled at Philip. 'Yes – but I hope

you're not going to be as noisy as this all the time. Bill, you'll have to protect me from this rowdy crowd of children.'

'I'll protect you all right,' promised Bill, swinging the car round another bend. 'I'll knock all their heads together once a day at least – and if Lucy-Ann starts getting tough with me I'll . . .'

'Oh *Bill*! said Lucy-Ann, the youngest and least boisterous of the lot. 'Jack's always saying I'm not tough *enough*. I ought to be by now, though, considering all the adventures I've been through.'

'Tough enough, tough enough!' chanted Kiki the parrot, who loved words that sounded alike. 'Tough enough, tough . . .'

'Oh, stop her,' groaned Mrs Mannering. She was tired with their long car journey, and was hoping it would soon be over. She had eight weeks of the children's holidays before her, and was quite sure she would be worn out before the end of it.

Philip and Dinah were her own children, and Jack and Lucy-Ann, who had no parents, lived with her in the holidays and loved her as if she were their own mother. Bill Cunningham was their very good friend, and had had some hair-raising adventures with them.

He had come with them on these holidays to keep them out of any more adventures – or so he said! Mrs Mannering vowed she was not going to let them out of her sight for eight weeks, unless Bill was with them –

then they couldn't possibly disappear, or fall into some dreadful new adventure.

'They ought to be safe, tucked away in the Welsh mountains, with both you and me, Bill, to look after them,' said Mrs Mannering. Mr Mannering had been dead for many years and Mrs Mannering often found it difficult to cope with so many lively children at once, now that they were growing older.

Philip loved any animal, bird or insect. His sister Dinah didn't share this love at all, and disliked most wild animals, and hated quite a number of harmless insects, though she was certainly better than she used to be. She was a hot-tempered girl, as ready to use her fists as Philip, and they had many a battle, much to gentle Lucy-Ann's dismay.

Lucy-Ann and Jack were brother and sister too. Kiki the parrot was Jack's beloved parrot, usually to be found on his shoulder. In fact, Mrs Mannering had once actually suggested that she should put a little leather patch on the shoulders of each of Jack's coats to stop Kiki from wearing thin places there with her clawed feet.

Jack was fond of birds, and he and Philip spent many an exciting hour together bird-watching, or taking photographs. They had a marvellous collection of these, which Bill said was worth a lot of money. They had brought cameras with them on this holiday, and, of course, their field-glasses for watching birds at a distance.

'We might see eagles again,' said Jack. 'Do you

remember the eagle's nest we found near that old castle in Scotland once, Philip? We might see buzzards too.'

'Buzz-z-z-z-z,' said Kiki at once. 'Buzz! Buzz off!'

'We might even have an adventure,' said Philip, with a grin. 'Though Mother and Bill are quite certain they will guard us from even the smallest one this time!'

Now here they were, all set for a wonderful holiday in the Welsh mountains, in a very lonely spot, where they could wander about with cameras and field-glasses wherever they liked. Each child was to have a donkey, so that they could ride along the narrow mountain paths as much as they wished.

'I shan't always come with you,' said Mrs Mannering, 'because I'm not so thrilled with donkey-riding as you are. But Bill will be with you, so you'll be safe.'

'Ah – but will Bill be safe with *us*?' said Jack, with a grin. 'We always seem to drag him into something or other. Poor Bill!'

'If you manage to pull me into an adventure in the middle of some of the loneliest of the Welsh mountains, you'll be clever,' said Bill.

The car swung round another bend and a farmhouse came into sight.

'We're nearly there,' said Mrs Mannering. 'I believe I can see the farmhouse we're going to stay at. Yes – there it is.'

The children craned their necks to see it. It was a

rambling old stone place, set on the mountain-side, with barns and out-buildings all around. In the evening sun-set it looked welcoming and friendly.

'Lovely!' said Lucy-Ann. 'What's it called?'

Bill said something that sounded like 'Doth-goth-oo-elli-othel-in.'

'Gracious!' said Dinah. 'What a name! Not even Kiki could pronounce that, I'm sure. Tell her it, Bill. See what she says.'

Bill obligingly told the name to the parrot, who listened solemnly and raised her crest politely.

'Now you just repeat that,' said Jack to Kiki. 'Go on!'

'This-is-the-house-that-Jack-built,' said the parrot, running all the words together. The children laughed.

'Good try, Kiki!' said Jack. 'You can't stump Kiki, Bill – she'll always say something. Good old Kiki!'

Kiki was pleased by this praise, and made a noise like the car changing gear. She had been doing this at intervals during the whole of the journey and had nearly driven Mrs Mannering mad.

'*Don't* let Kiki start that again,' she begged. 'Thank goodness we are here at last! Where's the front door, Bill – or isn't there one?'

There didn't seem to be one. The track went up to what appeared to be a barn and stopped there. A small path then ran to the farmhouse, divided into three and went to three different doors.

The children tumbled out of the car. Bill got out and stretched his legs. He helped Mrs Mannering out and they all looked round. A cock near by crowed and Kiki promptly crowed too, much to the cock's astonishment.

A plump, red-faced woman came hurrying out of one of the doors, a welcoming smile on her face. She called behind her to someone in the house.

'Effans, Effans, they have come, look you, they have come!'

'Ah – Mrs Evans,' said Bill, and shook hands with her. Mrs Mannering did the same. A small man came running out of the house, and came up to them too.

'This iss Effans, my husband,' said the plump woman. 'We hope you will be very happy with us, whateffer!'

This was said in a pleasant sing-song voice that the children liked very much. Everybody shook hands solemnly with Mrs Evans and her husband, and Kiki held out a claw as well.

'A parrot, look you!' cried Mrs Evans to her husband. 'Effans, a parrot!'

Mr Evans didn't seem to like the look of Kiki as much as his wife did, but he smiled politely.

'It iss very welcome you are,' he said in his sing-song voice. 'Will you pleass to come this way?'

They all followed Effans. He led them to the farmhouse, and, when the door was flung open, what a welcome sight met the children's eyes!

A long, sturdy kitchen table was covered with a snow-white cloth, and on it was set the finest meal the children had ever seen in their lives.

A great ham sat ready to be carved. A big tongue garnished round with bright green parsley sat by its side. An enormous salad with hard-boiled eggs sprinkled generously all over it was in the middle of the table. Two cold roast chickens were on the table too, with little curly bits of cold bacon set round.

The children's eyes nearly fell out of their heads. What a feast! And the scones and cakes! The jams and the pure yellow honey! The jugs of creamy milk!

'I say – are you having a party or something?' asked Jack, in awe.

'A party! No, no – it is high tea for you, look you,' said Mrs Evans. 'We cannot do dinners for you at night, we are busy people! You shall have what we have, and that is all. Here is high tea for you today, and when you have washed, it iss ready!'

'Oh – have we got to wash?' said Philip with a sigh. 'I'm clean enough. Golly, look at that meal! I say, if we're going to have food like this these hols I shan't want to go donkey-riding at all. I'll just stay here and eat!'

'Well, if you do that you'll be too fat for any donkey to carry,' said his mother. 'Go and wash, Philip. Mrs Evans will show us our rooms – we can all do with a wash and a brush – and then we can do justice to this magnificent meal.'

Up some narrow winding stairs went the little party, into big low-ceilinged rooms set with heavy old-fashioned furniture. Mrs Evans proudly showed them a small bathroom, put in for visitors to the farmhouse.

There were four rooms for the party. Bill had a small one to himself. Mrs Mannering had a big one, well away from the children's rooms, because they were often so noisy in the mornings. Philip and Jack had a curious little room together, whose ceiling slanted almost to the floor, and the girls had a bigger one next door.

'Isn't this going to be fun?' said Jack, scrubbing his hands vigorously in the bathroom, whilst Kiki sat on a tap. 'I'm longing to get at that meal downstairs. What a spread!'

'Move up,' said Dinah impatiently. 'There's room for two at this basin. We shall have to take it in turns to come in in the morning. Oh, Kiki, don't fly off with the nail-brush! Jack, stop her.'

The nail-brush was rescued and Kiki was tapped on the beak. She didn't mind. She was looking forward to the food downstairs as much as the children. She had seen a bowl of raspberries which she meant to sit as near to as possible. She flew to Jack's shoulder and muttered loving things into his ear whilst he dried his hands on a very rough towel.

'Stop it, Kiki. You tickle,' said Jack. 'Are you ready,

you others? Aunt Allie! Bill! Are you ready? We're going downstairs.'

'Coming!' cried the others, and down they all went. Now for a proper feast!

2

At the farmhouse

That first meal in the Welsh farmhouse was a very happy one. Mrs Evans was excited to have visitors, and Effans, her husband, beamed all round as he carved great slices of ham, tongue and chicken. There were a lot of 'look yous' and 'whateffers', and Kiki was especially interested in the up-and-down song-like way the two Welsh folk talked.

'Wipe your feet, whateffer,' she said to Mrs Evans suddenly. Mrs Evans looked surprised. She hadn't heard the parrot speak before.

'Shut the door, look you,' commanded Kiki, raising her crest. The children squealed with laughter.

'She's speaking Welsh already!' said Dinah. 'Hey, watch her, Jack – she's absolutely wolfing those raspberries!'

Jack put a plate over the bowl, and Kiki was angry. She made a noise like the car changing gear and Effans looked startled.

'It's all right – it's only Kiki,' said Jack. 'She can make all kinds of noises. You should hear her give her imitation of a train whistling in a tunnel.'

Kiki opened her beak and swelled up her throat as if she was about to make this horrible noise. Mrs Mannering spoke hastily. 'Jack! Don't let Kiki make that noise. If she does you'll have to take her upstairs and put her in your bedroom.'

'Bad Kiki, naughty Kiki,' said the parrot solemnly, recognizing the stern tone in Mrs Mannering's voice. She flew to Jack's shoulder and cuddled there, eyeing the plate that he had put over the bowl of raspberries. She gave his ear a little nip.

What a meal that was for six very hungry travellers who had had nothing but sandwiches all day long! Even Mrs Mannering ate more than she had ever eaten before at one meal. Mrs Evans kept beaming round as she filled the plates.

'There iss plenty more in the larder, look you,' she said. 'Effans, go fetch the meat-pie.'

'No, no!' said Mrs Mannering. 'Please don't. We have more than enough here – it's only that we are extra hungry and the food is so very very good.'

Mrs Evans was pleased. 'It iss plain country food, but it iss very good for the children,' she said. 'They will soon have good appetites in this mountain air, look you.'

'Indeed to gootness they will,' agreed Effans. 'Their appetites are small yet. They will grow.'

Mrs Mannering looked rather alarmed. 'Good gracious! I've never in my life seen them eat so much – if their appetites get any bigger I'll never be able to feed them at home!'

'And we shall *starve* at school,' grinned Jack.

'The poor boy!' said Mrs Evans. 'It iss a big ham I must give him to take back, whateffer!'

At last nobody could eat any more. They sat back from the table, looking out of the wide, low windows and the big open door. What a view!

Great mountains reared up their heads in the evening light. Deep shadows lay across the valley, but the mountains still caught the sunlight, and gleamed enchantingly. It was all so different from the country round their home, and the children felt that they could never look long enough on the mountain-tops and the shadowed valleys below.

'You are very lonely here,' said Bill. 'I can't see a single house or farm anywhere.'

'My brother lives on the other side of that mountain,' said Mrs Evans, pointing. 'I see him at the market each week. That is ten miles away, or maybe eleven. And my sister lives beyond that mountain you can see there. She too has a farm. So we have neighbours, you see.'

'Yes – but not next-door ones!' said Dinah. 'Don't you ever feel cut-off and lonely here, Mrs Evans?'

Mrs Evans looked surprised. 'Lonely? Indeed to gootness, what iss there to be lonely about, with Effans by my side, and the shepherd up on the hills, and the cow-herd and his wife in their cottage near by? And there iss plenty of animals, as you will see.'

Hens wandered in and out of the open door, pecking up crumbs fallen from the table. Kiki watched them intently. She began a warm, clucking noise, and the hens clucked back. A cock came strutting in and looked round for the hen that had a cluck he didn't quite know.

'Cock-a-doodle-doo!' suddenly crowed the cock defiantly, catching sight of Kiki on Jack's shoulder.

'Cock-a-doodle-doo!' answered Kiki, and the cock immediately jumped up on to the table to fight the crowing parrot.

He was shooed down and ran out indignantly, followed by a cackle of laughter from Kiki. Effans held his sides and laughed till the tears ran down his cheeks.

'That is a fine bird, look you!' he said to Jack, quite losing his heart to Kiki. 'Let her help herself to the raspberries again.'

'She's had enough, thank you very much,' said Jack, pleased at Effans' praise of Kiki. People sometimes didn't like the parrot, and when she went away with him Jack was always anxious in case anyone should object to her.

They all wandered out into the golden evening air, happy and well satisfied. Bill and Mrs Mannering sat on an old stone wall, watching the sun sink behind a mountain in the west. The four children went round the farmhouse and its buildings.

'Pigs! And what a marvellous clean pig-sty,' said Dinah. 'I've never seen a clean pig before. Look at this one, fat and shining as if it's been scrubbed.'

'It probably has, in preparation for our coming!' said Philip. 'I love these little piglets too. Look at them rooting round with their funny little snouts.'

'Kiki will soon have a wonderful collection of noises,' said Lucy-Ann, hearing the parrot giving a very life-like grunt. 'She'll be able to moo and bellow and grunt and crow and cluck . . .'

'And gobble like a turkey!' said Dinah, seeing some turkeys near by. 'This is a lovely farm. They've got everything. Oh, Philip – *look* at that kid!'

There were some goats on the mountain-side not far off, and with them was a kid. It was snow-white, dainty and altogether lovely. Philip stood looking at it, loving it at once.

He made a curious little bleating noise and all the goats looked round and stopped eating. The kid pricked up its little white ears, and stood quivering on its slender legs. It was very young and new.

Philip made the noise again. The kid left its mother and came leaping to him. It sprang right into his arms and nestled there, butting its soft white head against Philip's chin.

'Oh, Philip – isn't it sweet!' said the girls, and stroked the little thing and rubbed their cheeks against its snow-white coat.

'I wish animals came to me like they come to you, Philip,' said Lucy-Ann enviously. It was amazing the attraction that Philip had for creatures of any kind. Even a moth would rest contentedly on his finger, and the number of strange pets he had had was unbelievable. Hedgehogs, stag-beetles, lizards, young birds, mice, rats – you never knew what Philip would have next. All creatures loved him and trusted him, and he in turn understood them and loved them too.

'Now this kid will follow at his heels like a dog the whole time we're here,' said Dinah. 'Well, I'm glad it will be a kid, not a cow! Do you remember that awful time when Philip went into a field with a herd of cows in, and they all went to him and nuzzled him and followed him about like dogs. They even tried to get over the gate and through the hedge when he went out. I was awfully scared they would.'

'You ought to be ashamed of being afraid of cows,' said Philip, stroking the kid. 'There's no reason to be, Di. It's surprising you're not afraid of this kid. I bet you'd run if the goats came near.'

'I shouldn't,' said Dinah indignantly, but all the same she moved off hurriedly when the herd of goats, curious at seeing the kid in Philip's arms, began to come nearer to the children.

Soon they were all round Philip, Lucy-Ann and Jack. Dinah watched from a distance. The kid bleated when it saw its mother, but as soon as Philip put the little thing down to run to her, it leapt straight back into his arms!

'Well! You'll have to take it to bed with you tonight, there's no doubt about that,' said Jack, grinning. 'Come on – let's go and see the horses. They're the kind with shaggy hooves – I just love those!'

The goats were shooed off, and the children went to look at the great horses standing patiently in the field. There were three of them. They all came to Philip at once of course.

He had put down the little kid, and now it followed so close to his heels that, every time he stopped, it ran into his legs. At the first possible chance it sprang into his arms again. It followed him into the farmhouse too.

'Oh! You have found little Snowy!' said Mrs Evans, looking round from her oven with a face redder than ever. 'He has not left his mother before, look you!'

'Oh, Philip, don't bring the kid in here,' said Mrs Mannering, seeing at once that yet another animal had attached itself to Philip. She was afraid that Mrs Evans would object strongly to the kid coming indoors with Philip – and once it had felt the boy's attraction nothing would stop it from following him anywhere – even upstairs!

'Oh, it iss no matter if a kid comes into the house,' said Mrs Evans. 'We haff the new-born lambs in, and the hens are always in and out, and Moolie the calf used to come in each day before she was put in the field.'

The children thought it was a wonderful idea to let creatures wander in and out like that, but Mrs Mannering thought differently. She wondered if she would find eggs laid in her bed, or a calf in her bedroom chair! Still, it was a holiday, and if Mrs Evans like creatures wandering all over her kitchen, the children would like it too!

Lucy-Ann gave an enormous yawn and sank down into a big chair. Mrs Mannering looked at her, and then at the grandfather clock ticking in a corner.

'Go to bed, all of you,' she said. 'We're all tired. Yes, I know it's early, Philip, you don't need to tell me that – but we've had a long day, and this mountain air is very strong. We shall all sleep like tops tonight.'

'I will get ready some creamy milk for you,' began Mrs Evans, 'and you would like some buttered scones and jam to take up with you?'

'Oh, *no*,' said Mrs Mannering. 'We simply couldn't eat a thing more tonight, thank you, Mrs Evans.'

'Oh, *Mother*! Of *course* we could eat scones and jam and drink some more of that heavenly milk,' said Dinah indignantly. So they each took up a plate of scones and raspberry jam and a big glass of creamy milk to have in bed.

There came the scampering of little hooves, and Snowy the kid appeared in the boys' bedroom. He leapt in delight on to Philip's bed.

'Gosh! Look at this! Snowy's come upstairs!' said Philip. 'Have a bit of scone, Snowy?'

'I say – did we hear the kid coming up the stairs?' said Lucy-Ann, putting her head round the door of the boys' room. 'Oooh, Philip! You've got him on your bed!'

'Well, he won't get off,' said Philip. 'As soon as I push him off, he's on again – look! Like a puppy!'

'Maa-aa-aa!' said the kid in a soft, bleating voice, and butted Philip with its head.

'Are you going to have it up here all the night?' asked Dinah, appearing in her pyjamas.

'Well, if I put it outside, it'll only come in again – and if I shut the door it will come and butt it with its head,' said Philip, who had quite lost his heart to Snowy. 'After all, Jack has Kiki in the room with him all night.'

'Oh, *I* don't mind you having Snowy,' said Dinah. 'I just wondered what Mother would say, that's all – and Mrs Evans.'

'I shouldn't be at all surprised to hear that Mrs Evans has got a sick cow in her room, and half a dozen hens,' said Philip, arranging Snowy in the crook of his knees. 'She's a woman after my own heart. Go away, you girls. I'm going to sleep. I'm very happy – full of scones and jam and milk and sleep.'

Kiki made a hiccuping noise. 'Pardon!' she said. This was a new thing she had learnt from somebody at Jack's school the term before. It made Mrs Mannering cross.

'I should think Kiki's full up too,' said Jack sleepily.

'She pinched a whole scone, and I'm sure she's been at the raspberries again. Look at her beak! Now shut up, Kiki, I want to go to sleep.'

'Pop goes the weasel, look you,' said Kiki solemnly and put her head under her wing. The girls disappeared. The boys fell asleep. What a lovely beginning to a summer holiday!

3

The first morning

The next day the two girls awoke first. It was early, but
somebody was already about in the yard. Lucy-Ann
peeped out of the window.

'It's Effans,' she said. 'He must have been milking.
Dinah, come here. Did you ever see such a glorious view
in your life?'

The two girls knelt at the window. The sun was
streaming across the valley below through the opening
between two mountains, but the rest of the vale was in
shadow. In the distance many mountains reared their
great heads, getting bluer and bluer the further they were
away. The sky was blue without a cloud.

'Holiday weather – real holiday weather!' said Dinah
happily. 'I hope Mother lets us go picnicking today.'

'There's one thing about *this* holiday,' said Lucy-Ann,
'we shan't have any awful adventures, because Aunt Allie
is absolutely determined to go with us, or send Bill with
us, wherever we go.'

'Well, we've had our share of adventures,' said Dinah, beginning to dress. 'More than most children ever have. I don't mind if we don't have one this time. Hurry, Lucy-Ann, then we can get to the bathroom before the boys. Don't make too much row because Mother doesn't want to be wakened too early.'

Lucy-Ann popped her head in at the boys' room on the way to the bathroom. They were still sound asleep. Kiki took her head from under her wing as she heard Lucy-Ann at the door, but she said nothing, only yawned. Lucy-Ann looked closely at Philip's bed.

Snowy the kid was still there, cuddled into the crook of Philip's knees! Lucy-Ann's heart warmed to Philip. What an extraordinary boy he was, to have every creature so fond of him, and to be able to do anything he liked with them. The little kid raised its head and looked at Lucy-Ann.

She fled to the bathroom and washed with Dinah. They soon heard the boys getting up, and Kiki's voice telling somebody to wipe his feet.

'She's probably teaching a few manners to Snowy,' giggled Lucy-Ann. 'Kiki always tries to teach things to all Philip's pets. Oh, Dinah – do you remember how funny she was with Huffin and Puffin, the two puffins we found when we had our last adventure?'

'Arr,' said Dinah, making the noise the puffins used to make. Kiki heard them. 'Arrrrr!' she called from the boys' bedroom. 'Arrrrr!' Then she went off into a cackle of laughter, and Snowy the kid stared at her in alarm.

'Maa-aa-aa!' said the kid.

'Maa-aa-aa!' said Kiki, and the kid looked all round for another kid. The boys laughed.

Kiki, always encouraged when people laughed, swelled up her throat to make the noise of a car changing gear, her favourite noise of the moment, but Philip stopped her hurriedly.

'Stop it, Kiki! We've had enough of that noise. Do forget it!'

'God save the Queen!' said Kiki, in a dismal voice. 'Wipe your feet, blow your nose.'

'Come on,' said the girls, putting their heads in. 'Slowcoaches!'

They all went downstairs just as Mrs Evans was setting the last touches to the breakfast-table. It was loaded almost as much as the supper-table the night before. Jugs of creamy milk stood about the table, warm from the milking, and big bowls of raspberries had appeared again.

'I shan't know what to have,' groaned Jack, sitting down with Kiki on his shoulder. 'I can smell eggs and bacon – and there's cereal to have with raspberries and cream – and ham – and tomatoes – and gosh, is that cream cheese? Cream cheese for breakfast, how super!'

Snowy the kid tried to get on to Philip's knee as he sat down to breakfast. He pushed him off. 'No, Snowy, not at meal-times. I'm too busy then. Go and say good morning to your mother. She must wonder where you are.'

Kiki was at work on the raspberries. Mrs Evans had actually put a plate aside for Kiki's own breakfast. She and Effans beamed at the bird. They both thought she was wonderful.

'Look you, whateffer!' said Kiki, and dipped her beak into the raspberries again. It was rapidly becoming pink with the juice.

The children had an extremely good meal before Bill or Mrs Mannering came down. The Evans' had had theirs already – in fact they seemed to have done a day's work, judging by the list of things that Evans talked about – he had cleaned out the pigs, groomed the horses, milked the cows, fetched in the eggs, been to see the cow-herd and a dozen other things besides.

'Mrs Evans, do you know where the donkeys are that we arranged to have, for riding in the mountains?' asked Philip, when he had finished his breakfast and Snowy was once more in his arms.

'Ah, Trefor the shepherd will tell you,' said Mrs Evans. 'It iss his brother, look you, that has the donkeys. He is to bring them here for you.'

'Can't we go and fetch them and ride them back?' said Jack.

'Indeed to gootness, Trefor's brother lives thirty miles away!' said Effans. 'You could not walk there, whateffer.

You go and see Trefor today and ask him what has he done about your donkeys.'

Mrs Mannering and Bill appeared at that moment, looking fresh and trim after their good night's sleep in the sharp mountain air.

'Any breakfast left for us?' said Bill with a grin.

Mrs Evans hurried to fry bacon and eggs again, and soon the big kitchen was full of the savoury smell.

'Golly, if I stay here and smell that I shall feel hungry all over again,' said Philip. 'Bill, we're going up to see Trefor the shepherd to ask about our donkeys. Mother, can we have a picnic in the mountains as soon as the donkeys come?'

'Yes – when I'm sure I can keep on my donkey all right,' said his mother. 'If mine's a very fat donkey I shall slide off!'

'They are not fat,' Effans assured her. 'They are used in the mountains and they are strong and small. Sometimes we use ponies, but Trefor's brother breeds donkeys, and they are just as good.'

'Well, we'll go and have a talk with Trefor,' said Philip, getting up and letting Snowy fall off his knee. 'Come on, everyone! Kiki, do you want to be left with the raspberries? You greedy bird!'

Kiki flew to Jack's shoulder, and the party set off up the path that Effans had pointed out to them. Snowy bounded with them, turning a deaf ear to his mother's bleats. Already he seemed one of the company, petted by them all, though Kiki was not altogether pleased to have another creature taking up so much of the children's attention.

They went up the steep little path. The sun was up higher now and was hot. The children wore only thin blouses or shirts, and shorts, but they felt very warm. They came to a spring gushing out of the hillside and sat down to drink, and to cool their hands and feet. Snowy drank too, and then capered about lightly on his strong little legs, leaping from place to place almost as if he had wings.

'I wish I could leap like a goat,' said Jack lazily. 'It looks so lovely and easy to spring up high into the air like that, and land wherever you want to.'

Philip suddenly made a grab at something that was slithering past him on the warm bank. Dinah sat up at once. 'What is it, what is it?'

'This,' said Philip, and showed the others a silvery-grey, snake-like creature, with bright little eyes.

Dinah screamed at once. 'A snake! Philip, put it down. Philip, it'll bite you.'

'It won't,' said Philip calmly. 'It's not a snake – and anyway British snakes don't bite unless they're adders. I've told you that before. This is a slow-worm – and a very fine specimen too!'

The children looked in fascination as the silvery slow-worm wriggled over Philip's knees. It certainly looked very like a snake, but it wasn't. Lucy-Ann and Jack knew that, but Dinah always forgot. She was so terrified of snakes that to her anything that glided along must belong to the snake family.

'It's horrible,' she said with a shudder. 'Let it go, Philip. How do you know it's not a snake?'

'Well – for one thing it blinks its eyes and no snake does that,' said Philip. 'Watch it. It blinks like a lizard – and no wonder, because it belongs to the lizard family.'

As he spoke the little creature blinked its eyes. It stayed still on Philip's knee and made no further attempt to escape. Philip put his hand over it and it stayed there quite happy.

'I've never had a slow-worm for a pet,' said Philip. 'I've a good mind . . .'

'Philip! If you dare to keep that snake for a pet I'll tell Mother to send you home!' said Dinah in great alarm.

'Dinah, it's *not* a snake!' said Philip impatiently. 'It's a lizard – a legless lizard – quite harmless and very interesting. I'm going to keep it for a pet if it'll stay with me.'

'Stay with you! Of course it will,' said Jack. 'Did you ever know an animal that wouldn't? I should hate to go to a jungle with you, Philip – you'd have monkeys hanging lovingly round your neck, and tigers purring at you, and snakes wrapping themselves round your legs, and . . .'

Dinah gave a little scream. 'Don't say such horrible things! Philip, make that slow-worm go away.'

Instead he slipped it into his pocket. 'Now don't

worry, Dinah,' he said. 'You don't need to come near me. I don't expect it will stay with me because it won't like my pocket – but I'll just see.'

They set off up the hill once more, Dinah hanging back carefully. Oh dear! Philip *would* go and spoil the holiday by keeping something horrible again!

4

Up on the mountain-side

Trefor the shepherd had a small cabin-like cottage a good way up the mountain-side. Around him for miles grazed the sheep. Nearer in were that year's lambs, now grown into sturdy little beasts, their woolly coats showing up against the sheared bodies of the older sheep.

The shepherd was having a simple meal when they got to his hut. He had bread, butter, cream cheese and onions, and beside him a great jug of milk that he had cooled by standing it in the stream that ran down the mountain-side near by.

He nodded his head to the children as they came up. He was a curious-looking old fellow, with longish untidy hair, a straggling beard, and two of the brightest blue eyes the children had ever seen.

He spoke Welsh, which they didn't understand. 'Can you speak English?' asked Jack. 'We can't understand what you say.'

Trefor knew a few words of English, which, after much thought and munching of onions, he spoke.

'Donkeys. Tomorrow.'

He added something the children didn't understand, and waved his hand down the mountain-side towards the farmhouse.

'He means the donkeys will arrive tomorrow at the farm,' said Jack. 'Good! Perhaps Aunt Allie and Bill will come for a picnic on the donkeys.'

Trefor was very interested in Kiki. He had never in his life seen a parrot. He pointed at Kiki and laughed a hoarse laugh. Kiki at once copied it.

Trefor looked startled. 'Wipe your feet,' said Kiki sternly. 'How many times have I told you to shut the door? Three blind mice!'

Trefor stared at the parrot, amazed. Kiki cackled loudly. 'Look you, whateffer, look you, whateffer, look . . .'

The children laughed. Jack tapped Kiki on the beak. 'Now, now, Kiki – don't show off.'

Snowy butted against Philip's legs. He didn't like so much attention being given to Kiki. Philip turned, and the little creature leapt straight into his arms. Trefor seemed most amused and sent out a flood of Welsh words that nobody could understand at all. He tapped Philip on the arm, and then pointed to the ground to show the children that he wanted them to sit down.

They sat down, wondering what he wanted. He went

a little way down the hillside, making a soft baaing noise. From everywhere around the woolly lambs looked up. They came running to the shepherd, bleating, and even little Snowy left Philip and ran too. The shepherd knelt down and the lambs crowded round him, nuzzling against him. Trefor had had them when they were tiny – he had looked after them, even fed some of them from bottles if their mothers had died – and when they heard his soft call that once they had known so well, they remembered and came to him, their first friend.

A lump came into Lucy-Ann's throat. There was something very touching in the sight of that solemn, lonely, long-haired old shepherd, calling to his lambs and being answered. Snowy the kid, eager to get close to him, leapt on to the woolly backs of the lambs, and butted his head against him.

'Look at Snowy! Isn't he a cheeky rascal of a kid!' said Dinah. 'My goodness, you can hardly see Trefor now, he's so surrounded by lambs!'

Trefor came back, smiling, his eyes very blue in his old brown face. He offered the children some bread and onions, but the onions were big and strong-smelling, and Jack felt certain Mrs Mannering wouldn't approve if they all came back smelling strongly of Trefor's onions.

'No, thank you,' he said politely. 'Will you be down to see your brother tomorrow, when he brings the donkeys?'

Trefor seemed to understand this. He nodded. 'I come. Tomorrow. Donkeys.'

'Getting quite talkative, isn't he?' said Jack to the others. 'Right, Trefor. See you tomorrow then.'

They set off down the hill again. They stopped once more at the little spring to drink. They sat on the grass, looking at the towering mountains round them.

'Effans says that all those mountains over there have hardly anyone living on them, because they are difficult to get at,' said Jack. 'I bet there are some interesting animals and birds there. Wish we could go and see.'

'I don't see why we shouldn't if Bill and Mother would come with us,' said Philip, trying to stop Snowy from walking on his middle. 'Stop it, Snowy. Get off my tummy. Your hooves are sharp. It would be fun to go off into the mountains on donkeys and take food with us for a few days.'

'And have tents, do you mean?' said Jack. 'I say – that's an idea, Philip. We could take our cameras and get some fine pictures. I might see some rare birds.'

'I bet you would!' said Philip. 'Hallo, here comes Sally Slither!'

Out of his pocket glided the slow-worm, and curled itself up in the crook of Philip's elbow, in the sun. Dinah removed herself to a safe distance at once. Kiki looked down with interest from her perch on Jack's shoulder.

'Sally Slither! What a nice name!' said Lucy-Ann,

running her finger down the slow-worm's silvery back. 'Look – my finger's tickling her – she's going all dithery!'

'Slithery dithery,' said Kiki, at once. She had a real talent for putting together words of the same sound. 'Dithery slithery, slithery dithery . . .'

'All right, all right,' said Philip. 'We don't want to hear it again, Kiki. You're a clever old bird, we all know that. Jack, look at this slow-worm. It's not a scrap frightened now.'

'I do think you're mean to keep it,' began Dinah, from a safe distance. 'You know how I hate snakes. All right, all right, I *know* it isn't a snake – though I wouldn't be a bit surprised if it bit me if I came near it, so there!'

'I wouldn't be surprised at anything biting you when you're so nervous,' said Philip crossly. 'I feel like biting you myself. Come here, Dinah. Run your fingers down Sally Slither's back – look at her sharp little eyes . . .'

Dinah gave a scream. 'I couldn't bear it! No, don't come near me, Philip. It's worse than those awful white rats you had a few months ago. But at least they grew up and you let them go!'

'Sally can go whenever she wants to,' said Philip. 'I never keep any pet when it wants to go. Do you want to go, Sally Slither?'

'Slithery dithery, musty dusty fusty,' said Kiki, trying to remember the various collections of words she had picked up at one time or another. 'Huffin and Puffin.'

'Come on – let's go,' said Dinah. 'Perhaps that horrible thing will go back into your pocket if we go. And I'm getting hungry.'

The slow-worm slid back somewhere in Philip's clothes. He got up and Snowy bounded round him. 'Now just see if you can walk without getting your head between my legs all the time,' said Philip to Snowy. 'You'll send me flying in a minute. You're a bit *too* friendly at times, Snowy.'

They went back to the farmhouse, enjoying the sunshine and the constant breeze that blew over the mountain-side. By the time they reached the farm-house they were all terribly hungry, and visions of ham, chicken, salad and raspberries and cream kept coming into their minds.

Bill and Mrs Mannering had been for a walk too, but down the mountain, not up. They had been back for a little while, and were just beginning to wonder where the children were. Snowy went bounding up to them.

'He's a pet!' said Mrs Mannering. 'I suppose we shall have him at our heels the whole of this holiday now. It's a pity kids have to grow up into goats. Don't think you're going to take Snowy back home with you, Philip. I'm not going to have a goat in the garden, whilst you're at school, eating the vegetables out of the beds, and the clothes off the line!'

'Mother, Trefor says his brother will arrive at the farmhouse tomorrow with the donkeys,' said Philip. 'Can we each choose our own? How many will there be?'

'Yes, you can choose your own if you want to,' said Mrs Mannering. 'I don't know how many there will be – six, I suppose. I only hope I choose a sure-footed one!'

'They'll all be sure-footed,' said Jack. 'As sure-footed as goats. But not so leapy. I shouldn't care to ride one of these mountain goats, and find myself leaping about from rock to rock.'

'Good gracious, what a horrible thought!' said Mrs Mannering. 'I shall choose the quietest, staidest, placidest, best-tempered donkey of the lot – one without a single bound or leap in him.'

Everyone laughed. Effans came over to them, beaming to see them happy. 'It iss dinner-time,' he said. 'Mrs Effans has it ready.'

'I shall soon begin to talk in a sing-song voice myself,' said Lucy-Ann, getting up from the stone wall. 'Indeed to gootness I shall!'

They all laughed at the lilting way she spoke. Snowy galloped ahead into the kitchen. Mrs Evans didn't seem to mind at all, but she shooed him down when he leapt into a chair. A hen scuttled out from under the table. Kiki went up to a rafter, sat on a ham wrapped up in a cloth, and cocked her eye down to the table to see what fruit there was.

'Pop goes the weasel,' she announced, and made a popping noise like a cork coming out of a bottle. Effans looked up in admiration.

'Such a bird!' he said. 'Never have I seen such a bird, look you!'

Kiki began hiccuping, and Effans went off into a roar of laughter. Mrs Mannering frowned.

'Kiki! Stop that! How many times am I to tell you I don't like that noise?'

'How many times have I told you to wipe your feet?' retorted Kiki, and screeched. Effans almost died of laughter. Kiki began to show off, snapping her beak open and shut, putting her crest up and down and making peculiar noises.

'Kiki! Come here!' said Jack sternly, and Kiki flew down to his shoulder. Jack tapped her smartly on her beak. 'Any more nonsense from you and I'll shut you in the bedroom upstairs. Bad bird! Silly bird!'

'Poor Polly! Bad Polly!' said Kiki, and nipped Jack's ear. He smacked her on the beak again.

'Be quiet! Not another word!' he ordered. Kiki put her head under her wing in disgrace, and various whispering sounds came to everyone's ears. But nobody could hear what she said, though Effans strained his ears hopefully. What a bird! He wished he could have one like it.

The dinner was as good as the high tea and breakfast had been. The children set to work and Mrs Evans felt very pleased to see how much her good food was appreciated. She kept pressing second and third helpings on everyone, but soon even the boys could eat no more.

'There iss no four o'clock tea,' she kept saying. 'Nothing till six o'clock. So eat, look you, eat!'

'Dithery slithery,' announced Kiki suddenly, and Dinah gave a scream. The slow-worm was gliding out of Philip's sleeve! He pushed it back hurriedly, hoping that no one had seen it. Bill had. His sharp eyes had caught sight of it at once. He grinned.

'Another member added to the family?' he said. 'Very nice too! What with Snowy and Kiki and – er – Slithery, we look all set for a most interesting holiday.'

5

Arrival of the donkeys

The next excitement, of course, was the arrival of the donkeys. The children had waited expectantly for them all the following morning, not liking to go for a walk in case they missed the donkeys' arrival. Lucy-Ann saw them first.

She gave a yell that sent the slow-worm back into Philip's pocket, and startled Snowy so much that he leapt four feet in the air. Even Kiki jumped.

'The donkeys!' cried Lucy-Ann. 'There they come, look, up the mountain path.'

Soon all four children were tearing down the path to the donkeys. There were eight of them, strong, sturdy little creatures, with big bright eyes, and long tails that whisked the flies away. They were all grey, and their long ears twitched to and fro as they came steadily up the steep path.

Trefor's brother David was with them, an elderly man rather like Trefor but with tidier hair and beard. He had the same bright blue eyes, but he looked timid and shy, as if the world had not been kind to him.

He smiled faintly at the lively children. 'Can we ride four of the donkeys now?' asked Philip. 'We know how to ride. Come on, Lucy-Ann, up with you!'

He gave Lucy-Ann a shove and she was up on a donkey's back. Dinah needed no help. With a leap like Snowy's she was up at once.

The donkeys ambled up the steep path with the children, refusing to trot now that they had heavy weights on their backs. Snowy galloped beside Philip's donkey, half jealous of it, butting it in the legs.

'Hallo! Here we are!' cried Jack, ambling up to Mrs Mannering and Bill. 'Eight donkeys to choose from! Which are you going to have, Aunt Allie?'

David stood by smiling whilst his donkeys were examined and tried. Trefor the shepherd arrived, and the two old brothers chatted together in Welsh. Effans and his wife came along, and soon there was quite a company in the farmyard, discussing the donkeys.

'We badly want to go off on the donkeys into the mountains, Mother,' said Philip coaxingly. 'Can we? With you and Bill, of course. To stay a few nights, I mean. Jack and I think there should be a fine lot of rare birds over there in those lonely mountains – and there will be lots of animals too.'

'It *would* be rather fun,' said his mother. 'I haven't

camped out for ages, and in this weather it would be lovely. What do you say, Bill?'

'I say yes!' said Bill, who loved outdoor life and was an old hand at camping. 'Do you good, Allie. We could take a couple of extra donkeys to carry the things we want.'

'Oh, *Bill!* Can we really go?' said Lucy-Ann, over-joyed, and Dinah danced round him too. To go off on donkeys into the mountains, and take tents and food – what could be more fun?

'It will be an adventure!' said Dinah. 'Not one of our usual ones, of course, but a really nice one. You'll like that, Lucy-Ann, won't you?'

'Oh, *yes,*' said Lucy-Ann, who never really enjoyed a proper adventure whilst it was happening. 'I'd like *that* kind of adventure. When can we go?'

'Well, we'd better get used to our donkeys before we think of going,' said Bill. 'I'm not used to donkey-riding, nor is Aunt Allie. We shall be stiff at first, so we'd better get over that stage before we go. Say next week?'

'Oh – I can't wait that long!' said Dinah, and the others laughed at her long face.

'Effans, where is a nice place to go?' asked Jack, turn-ing to him. Effans considered. He spoke to Trefor in Welsh and the old shepherd answered him.

'He says the Vale of Butterflies in a good place,' said Effans. 'It is full of birds as well as butterflies.'

'The Vale of Butterflies – that sounds gorgeous,' said Jack, pleased.

'Super!' said Philip. 'Absolutely wizard! We'll go there. Is it far?'

'Two days on donkeys,' said Effans.

Bill calculated. 'We shall want a guide – either Trefor, Effans or Trefor's brother – and two donkeys at least to carry our tents and food – and six donkeys for ourselves. That's nine. We've only got eight here. Effans, ask this fellow if he's got another donkey.'

It turned out that Trefor's brother had meant to ride home on a donkey himself, and take another donkey back with farm produce to sell, leaving only six. Effans bargained with him to come back the next week, complete with three donkeys to add to the six left behind.

'Then you can act as guide to these people, look you,' he said. 'That will be money. You will have one donkey, they will have six, and there will be two for loads. That is much money for you, David, indeed to gootness!'

David agreed. He would come on the Wednesday of next week, bringing three donkeys to add to the six he would leave behind. Two to carry loads, one for himself, and six for the children, Mrs Mannering and Bill.

The children were very excited. They ran round the donkeys, patted them, rubbed their long noses and sat on their broad backs. The donkeys seemed to like all the fuss. They stood stolidly there, their tails whisking, following the children with their eyes. Snowy darted about, running under first one donkey and then another, acting like a mad thing.

Trefor helped his brother to load up a donkey with packages of all kinds. Heavier and heavier grew the load, but the donkey stood patiently, seeming not to mind at all. Then, eager to be gone, it suddenly brayed.

Kiki had never heard a donkey bray before and she sailed straight up into the air with fright.

'Ee-ore, ee-ore!' brayed the donkey, and stamped his foot.

'Gracious! Now I suppose Kiki will practise braying too,' said Jack. 'We shall have to stop her firmly if she does. It's bad enough from a donkey – but brays from Kiki would be frightful.'

The donkey was loaded at last. David mounted his sturdy little beast, said a polite goodbye to everyone and rode off down the path, the loaded donkey being led after him by a rope he held in his hand.

'Now we can choose our own donkeys!' said Lucy-Ann in delight. 'Aunt Allie – you choose first.'

'Well, they all look *exactly* alike to me!' said Mrs Mannering. Bill spoke to Effans, asking him if he knew which donkey was the quietest. Effans turned to Trefor.

Trefor knew. He pointed out a little creature with a patient expression in its eyes, and said a few words in Welsh.

'He says that is the one for you,' said Effans. 'It is quiet and good. Its name is Patience.'

'Oh, good – I'll choose her then,' said Mrs Mannering. 'This is mine, children – the one with the black mark on her forehead.'

'I want this one,' cried Lucy-Ann, pulling at a sturdy animal that threw his head back continually, and stamped now and then. 'I like him. What is his name, Trefor?'

Trefor said something nobody understood. Effans translated. 'His name is Clover. This one is Grayling, and that one is Dapple. The other two are Buttercup and Daisy.'

Lucy-Ann had Clover. Jack had Grayling, and Dinah had Dapple. Bill had Buttercup, and Philip had Daisy. Each of them was delighted with his or her own special donkey.

'Let's ride them now,' said Jack, mounting his little beast. 'Come on, Bill. Aunt Allie, get on. We'll go for our first ride now – up the path and back again.'

With Effans and his wife looking on in delight, the six rode off on their donkeys. They would not go fast uphill, and Bill warned each child not to try and make them. 'They'll trot coming down all right,' he said. 'But it's heavy going for them uphill, with our weight on their backs.'

It was great fun riding the grey donkeys up the steep mountain path. Mrs Mannering was nervous at first when she came to the rocky bits, but her donkey was as sure-footed as the others, and went steadily along on even the stoniest parts.

Bill rode close by in case Mrs Mannering needed help, but she didn't. The four children, of course, would have scorned any help. They were all used to riding horses, and the donkeys were very easy to manage.

'Now we'll turn back,' called Bill. So they all turned and went homewards. Snowy came too, of course, having leapt and bounded ahead of them all the way, apparently under the impression that he was leading them.

'That was fun,' said Lucy-Ann, as they trotted homewards, the donkeys going faster now that they were on a downhill road. Mrs Mannering didn't like the trotting so much as the ambling.

'My donkey is a very bumpy one,' she said to Bill. 'When I go down he comes up and when I go up he goes down, so we keep meeting with a bump!'

Everyone laughed. They were all sorry when they reached the farmhouse, for by that time they felt as if they could go trotting on for ever. But a meal was ready for them on the table, and Mrs Evans was beaming at the door, so they didn't lose much time in taking the donkeys to the field and carrying their harness to the stables.

'You'll be quite used to riding a donkey by next week,' Bill said to Mrs Mannering. 'By the time Wednesday comes you'll be ready to set off and you'll feel as if you'd ridden a donkey all your life!'

'Oh, yes, I'm sure I shall,' said Mrs Mannering. She

felt something pecking at her foot and looked under the table. She saw a fat brown hen there and pushed it away. 'Shoo! Stop pecking my foot!'

The hen shooed, only to be replaced by Snowy, who, pushed off Philip's knee as he sat at table, was amusing himself by trying to eat shoe-laces under the table. Mrs Mannering pushed him him away too, and Snowy went to chew the hem of Mrs Evans' dress. She never noticed things like that, so Snowy had a nice long chew.

The next day the girls and Mrs Mannering were so stiff with their donkey-ride that they could hardly walk. The boys and Bill were all right, but Mrs Mannering groaned as she came down the stairs.

'Good gracious! I feel like an old old lady! I'll never be able to ride a donkey again!' she said.

But the stiffness wore off, and the six of them soon got used to riding their donkeys day after day into the mountains. There were some lovely rides and magnificent views. Snowy came with them always, never tired, leaping along gaily. Kiki rode on Jack's shoulder, occasionally taking a flight into the air to scare any bird that happened to be flying overhead. They flew off quickly, full of astonishment when Kiki told them to wipe their feet.

'Two days more and it's Wednesday,' said Lucy-Ann happily. 'We'll be quite ready then – able to ride for hours and hours.'

'Yes – off to the Vale of Butterflies!' said Jack. 'I

wonder what it's like! I imagine it to be full of wings of all colours. Lovely!'

'Oh, hurry up and come, Wednesday!' said Dinah. 'Only forty-eight hours – and then, off we go!'

But something unexpected happened in that forty-eight hours – something that quite upset their lovely plans!

6

Off to the Vale of Butterflies

It happened the very next day. It was when Mrs Mannering had gone with Mrs Evans to the big barn. The door suddenly blew shut, and caught her hand in it, trapping it tightly.

Mrs Mannering screamed. Mrs Evans ran to open the door, but poor Mrs Mannering's hand was badly bruised and crushed.

Bill was very concerned. 'I must take you down to the doctor,' he said. 'I'll get the car. Where are the children? Out on their donkeys? Tell them where we've gone, Mrs Evans, when they come back. They needn't worry. I'll have Mrs Mannering's hand seen to, and properly bandaged. I don't expect it will be very much, but I'd like her to have it X-rayed in case any small bone is broken.'

Looking rather white, Mrs Mannering was driven off by Bill, down the steep mountain road to the town that lay some way off in the next valley. It was about fifteen miles and soon Mrs Mannering was in hospital having her hand X-rayed and bound up.

The children were very upset when they heard what had happened. 'Poor Mother!' said Philip. 'It must have hurt dreadfully when her hand got caught in that heavy door.'

'Indeed to gootness, it did,' said Mrs Evans, who looked quite upset too. 'She gave one scream, poor soul, and then made not a sound, whateffer. Now don't look so sadly – she'll be back tonight.'

'Will she be able to go off to the mountains tomorrow?' asked Lucy-Ann. 'How can she ride with a bad hand?'

'Well, there now, she can't,' said Mrs Evans. 'But she can stay here with me and I'll look after her for you. You can go with Mr Cunningham and David.'

'But will Bill go if Mother's hurt?' wondered Philip. 'He thinks the world of her. Oh, blow! It's bad luck for this to happen just when we had such a lovely plan. Poor Mother! I do hope her hand's better now.'

Mrs Mannering arrived back in Bill's car that evening, just before high tea. She looked better, and made light of her hand.

'We've had it X-rayed,' said Bill. 'She's broken a tiny bone just here,' and he showed them where, on the back of his hand. 'It's got to be bandaged and kept at rest. I'm to take her down to have it seen again in three days' time.'

'I'm so sorry, dears,' said Mrs Mannering. 'And Bill, you don't need to take me down, you know. I'm quite able to drive myself down even with an injured hand. Take the children on their trip tomorrow. I can't bear to have them disappointed.'

'What! And leave you like this!' said Bill. 'Don't be silly, Allie. I shall take you down myself in the car on Friday. The children can go with David, if he'll take them on by himself. It's a perfectly ordinary trip, and they'll be back in a few days' time. They can all ride their donkeys as easily as David – and probably they'll enjoy a trip without us!'

'We'd *much* rather you and Aunt Allie came,' said Jack. 'But as you can't, it's decent of you to let us go alone. We'll be perfectly all right, Bill. David knows the way, and we can all look after ourselves.'

So it was settled that the four children should go by themselves on the donkeys with their guide David, taking with them tents, bedding and food. Philip questioned Bill to make sure that his mother's hand was not seriously hurt.

'Oh, no – it will soon be right,' said Bill. 'But I want to be sure she doesn't use it, and I want to take her down to the doctor in three days' time. I'm sorry not to come with you – but you'll be all right by yourselves. I don't see that you can get into any trouble, or any startling adventure, going donkey-riding in the mountains with David. Maybe we can all go together, later on.'

The children were very excited that night, getting ready the things they wanted to take. They had two small tents, a sleeping-bag each, two ground-sheets, cameras, field-glasses, a change of clothes – and food.

The food was Mrs Evans' care. Bill watched her packing up what she thought they would eat in the next few days.

'I didn't like to stop her,' he told the others. 'But, honestly, she's packed enough for a month. She's put in a whole ham!'

'Golly!' said Jack. 'What else?'

'A tongue or two, hard-boiled eggs, tins of all kinds, plum-cake and goodness knows what!' said Philip. 'We shall feast like kings.'

'Well,' began Lucy-Ann, 'I always think that we eat twice as much in the open air, because food tastes so . . .'

'Much nicer!' chorused everyone. Lucy-Ann always said that at least a dozen times each holidays. She laughed.

'Well, anyway, it will be nice to have as much as ever we can eat. There's David too – we've got to take food for him as well.'

'He doesn't look as if he'd eat much,' said Dinah. 'Skinny little fellow, he is!'

'You'd better go to bed early, children,' said Mrs Mannering a little later. 'You'll have a long ride tomorrow, according to Effans.'

'All right. It'll make tomorrow come all the sooner!' said Lucy-Ann. 'How's your hand feel, Aunt Allie?'

'It's quite comfortable, thank you,' said Mrs Mannering. 'I'm sure I could have gone with you tomorrow, really!'

'Well, you couldn't,' said Bill hastily, half afraid that Mrs Mannering would try to be foolish and go with the others after all. She laughed.

'Don't worry! I'm going to be sensible – and, dear me, it will be quite a change to be rid of four noisy ruffians and an even noisier bird for a few days, Bill, won't it?'

All the children were awake very early the next day. Snowy the kid, who was a real sleepy-head in the mornings, didn't want to wake up at all, and snuggled deeper into Philip's blankets as the boy tried to get out of bed.

Kiki took her head from under her wing and scratched her poll. 'Dithery Slithery,' she remarked, which meant that she had spied Philip's slow-worm. It was coiled up in a corner of the room. It would very much have liked to sleep on Philip's bed, but it was afraid of Snowy, who had a habit of nibbling anything near him.

The boys got up and looked out of the window. It was a really perfect day. The mountains towered up into the fresh morning sky, as beautiful as ever.

'They look as if someone had just been along and washed them,' said Jack. 'The sky looks washed too – so very very clean and new.'

'I like the feel of an early morning,' said Philip, putting on his shorts. 'It has a special *new* feel about it – as if it was the first morning that ever happened!'

Snowy went over to the corner where Sally the slow-worm was, and the slow-worm at once wriggled away under the chest of drawers. Philip picked her up and she slid gracefully into his pocket.

'Have to get you a few flies for breakfast, Sally,' said Philip. 'Shut up, Kiki – you'll wake the rest of the household with that awful cough.'

Kiki could give a terrible, hollow cough at times, which she had copied from an old uncle of Jack's, and she was practising it now. She stopped when Philip spoke to her, and hopped to Jack's shoulder.

'Funny bird, silly bird,' said Jack affectionately, scratching her neck. 'Come on, Philip – let's see if the girls are up.'

They were just getting up, both of them thrilled at the fine day and the idea of going camping in the mountains. 'Have you got that horrid slow-worm on you?' asked Dinah fearfully, looking at Philip.

'Yes, somewhere about,' said Philip, feeling all over him. 'There's one thing about Sally Slithery – she does get about!'

Dinah shuddered and went to wash in the bathroom. Snowy the kid was there, nibbling the cork bath-mat, which he evidently thought was delicious.

'Oh, Snowy! Mrs Evans won't be at all pleased with

you!' said Dinah, and shooed the kid out of the door. He went to find Philip. He was quite one of the family now.

Mrs Mannering's hand was stiff and sore that morning, but she said very little about it, not wanting to upset the children. She was glad it was such a lovely day for them, and watched with amusement as Mrs Evans carefully packed up all the food she had prepared for the children to take with them.

'If you eat all that you'll never be able to ride home on the donkeys,' she said. 'You'll be too fat.'

'They must not go hungry,' said kind Mrs Evans. 'There! I think I have thought of everything. Children, you must use one donkey for the food and the other for everything else, look you. I will see that David straps everything on well.'

The children listened to her kind, lilting voice as they sat at breakfast. They felt very happy, and the only thing that spoilt their pleasure was the fact that Bill and Mrs Mannering were not coming with them. On the other hand, they would be freer without grown-ups!

Kiki gave a hiccup, with one eye on Mrs Mannering. She looked at the parrot severely. 'Kiki! You did that on purpose. Do you want your beak smacked?'

'Pardon,' said Kiki, and went off into a cackle of laughter. Effans choked over his bacon, trying to laugh with his mouth full, and went purple in the face. His bacon went down the wrong way, and he got the hiccups too.

'Pardon, look you!' he said to Mrs Mannering, with such a horrified look on his face that everyone roared with laughter.

'Now here is David, all ready for you!' cried Mrs Evans from the door, where she had gone to chase away a turkey that had suddenly appeared. It made a gobbling noise that scared Snowy terribly. Kiki, of course, at once gobbled too, and the turkey looked into the kitchen in amazement. 'Shoo!' said Mrs Evans. 'Good morning, David, it's early you are, and a nice day you have brought with you!'

'Indeed to gootness I have,' said David and smiled timidly at the company in the big kitchen. His donkeys crowded round him, sturdy and patient, their harness clinking and glinting.

'Come on!' yelled Jack, suddenly feeling too excited to sit at the table any longer. 'Come on! Let's pack the things on the donkeys and go!'

They all rushed out. Soon David and Effans were strapping everything on two donkeys. One donkey had big panniers each side for food. The other had the things strapped across his broad little back. They stood perfectly still, their ears twitching as a fly or two settled on them.

'Well – are we ready to start?' said Philip. 'I think we've got everything. Oh, gosh, where are my field-glasses?'

At last everyone and everything was ready. It had been

explained to David that Bill and Mrs Mannering could not come, and Effans had said he would care for the two extra donkeys till the children came back. David did not seem too pleased to think he was to go alone with the children. He looked rather alarmed, Bill thought. Poor fellow! Bill wished it was Effans who was going with the children, not David. Still, the children were used to camping out and could be trusted to be sensible.

'Goodbye!' called everyone. 'See you in a few days' time. Take care of your hand, Mother! Now we're off – off to the Vale of Butterflies! Goodbye, everyone!'

7

On the way

With Bill, Mrs Mannering, Effans and Mrs Evans waving and calling goodbye, the party set off on their donkeys. They had to go up by Trefor the shepherd's little cabin, and the donkeys picked their way steadily up the steep hillside.

Snowy ran beside them, bobbing about under the donkeys' bodies as he pleased. They seemed to like him, and Dapple kept putting his head down to the kid whenever he came near. Kiki was perched as usual on Jack's shoulder, jogging up and down contentedly, snapping her beak, and making a few quiet remarks into Jack's ear.

They came to Trefor's cabin. He was on the hillside, seeing to a sick sheep. He came to meet them, his untidy hair blowing in the wind, and his eyes shining as blue as forget-me-nots.

There was a conversation between the two men in Welsh. David sounded rather complaining. Trefor seemed to be pooh-poohing what he said. David got out a map that Bill had given him, and appeared to be saying that he didn't understand it at all.

Trefor then spoke earnestly, pointing in this direction and that, poking David with his finger every time he wanted to make a point go home. The children thought he must be telling David the exact way to go.

'I hope David really does know the way,' said Jack. 'He might have thought Bill would help him with the map if Bill had been going. It looks to me as if he's telling Trefor he's not too certain of the way.'

'Well, what does it matter?' said Philip, pushing Snowy off with his hand as the kid tried to jump up on to his donkey with him. 'I'd *like* to see the Vale of Butterflies – but so long as we go off camping in those gorgeous mountains, that's all that matters.'

'Yes. We shall see heaps of birds and animals anyway,' said Jack, feeling that Philip was right. 'Come on, David! Let's go!'

David leapt on to his donkey at once. He called good-bye to Trefor, and the little company set off once more, taking a narrow path along the mountain-side that went neither very far up, nor very far down.

It was glorious riding there, so high, looking down on the valley far below. It was partly in the sun and partly in the shadow, for the sun was not yet high. Swallows flew round them catching flies, their steel-blue wings gleaming in the sun. Kiki watched them out of her sharp eyes. She had often tried fly-catching herself, but she knew she was no good at it. Anyway, flies didn't taste as good as fruit!

They ambled on until everyone felt hungry and thirsty. They came to a copse of birch-trees with a small stream near by.

'Let's picnic here,' said Philip, sliding off his donkey. 'In the shade of those trees. I'm absolutely cooked with the sun.'

David saw to the donkeys, taking them to the stream for water. He then let them wander free, for they came most obediently at his call, and could be trusted not to go too far away. They went to the shade of the trees and stood there, swishing their long grey tails, enjoying the rest.

Snowy ran to them, and behaved like a spoilt child, letting the donkeys fuss him and stare at him. Dapple put down his big head to the little kid, and nuzzled him in the neck. When Snowy ran to the next donkey Dapple followed him.

'Dapple wants to be friends with Snowy,' said Dinah, unpacking the lunch parcel from one of the enormous panniers. 'Here, Lucy-Ann – take this tin and fill it with water from the stream. It must be absolutely pure, I should think. We can put some of this lemonade essence with it. I'm so dreadfully thirsty!'

David was drinking at the stream, so the children felt that it must be all right. It gurgled along, fresh and clear, running through the pebbles and down the hillside at top speed. Lucy-Ann went to fill the tin.

There was a lovely lunch. The children had to call David to share it because he suddenly seemed shy. He came and sat down a little way away from them.

'No, David. Come here with us,' called Jack, patting the ground. 'We want to learn Welsh! Come and talk to us!'

But the old Welshman was very shy, and it was as much as the children could do to persuade him to eat his share of the lunch. It was such a good lunch too!

There were five different kinds of sandwiches, fresh lettuce wrapped in a damp cloth, hard-boiled eggs to nibble, and great slices of jam tart. Washed down with cold lemonade it was the finest lunch anyone could wish.

'Nobody in the whole world, not even the very richest king, can possibly have a nicer lunch than this,' said Lucy-Ann, munching a chicken sandwich.

'Or a nicer place to eat it in,' said Philip, waving his sandwich at the magnificent view before them. 'Look at that! No king could have a better view from his palace than that! Valleys and mountains, and yet more mountains, and then the clear blue sky! Marvellous!'

They all gazed at the unbelievable view that lay in front of them. A rustle of paper made them look round.

'Snowy! You greedy little kid! Look here, he's eaten the rest of the chicken sandwiches!' cried Jack indignantly, forgetting all about the lovely view. 'Philip, smack him. We can't let him do that or our food won't last out. He can jolly well eat the grass.'

Philip gave Snowy a smart tap on the nose. The kid retreated in a huff, taking with him a mouthful of sandwich papers, which he proceeded to eat with apparent enjoyment. But soon he was back with Philip, pressing against him affectionately, anxious to be back in his good books. Dapple the donkey moved over to Philip too, to be near the kid. He lay down beside him, and Philip at once leaned back against him.

'Thanks, old man! Very nice! Just what I wanted!' said Philip, and everyone laughed as he settled himself against the donkey's side.

'Have another sandwich, David?' asked Lucy-Ann, holding out a packet to him. David had not eaten nearly as much as they had, either through shyness or because he hadn't such an enormous appetite. He shook his head.

'Let's have a bit of rest now,' said Philip sleepily. 'There's no hurry. We can take all the time we like to get anywhere.'

Jack began to ask David the names of things in Welsh. It was silly not to be able to talk to David. David apparently understood more English than he spoke, but even the few English words he said were pronounced so differently that the children found it hard to puzzle out what he was saying.

'Come on, David, talk,' said Jack, who did not feel as

sleepy as the others. 'What's this in Welsh?' He held out his hand.

David began to realize that Jack wanted a lesson in Welsh, and he brightened up a little. He was a trifle embarrassed by Kiki, who insisted on repeating all the words he said too, and added a few nonsense words of her own for good measure.

The girls and Philip fell asleep in the shade, Lucy-Ann sharing Philip's donkey to lean against. Dinah would have liked to do the same but she was afraid that Sally the slow-worm might come out of Philip's pocket if she did, and nothing would make Dinah go near the silvery creature!

Jack patiently tried to learn a few Welsh words, and then got tired of it. He threw a few pebbles down the mountain-side, and gazed round at the many summits towering up in the distance. There was one odd one, shaped like three teeth, that amused him. He decided to look it up on the map.

The map, however, was rather disappointing. It showed very few names in the district where they were, probably because it had been very little visited, and there were no farmhouses or other buildings to put on record. Jack found a name that seemed to him to fit the mountain. 'Fang Mountain,' he read. 'That might be it. Gosh, what a lot of mountains there are about here! I bet nobody has ever explored them all. I'd like to fly over them in an aeroplane and look down on them. We haven't seen a plane since we've been here. Off the route, I suppose.'

David had gone to round up the donkeys. Jack woke up the others. 'Come on, lazy things! We'd better get on, or David will think we mean to camp here for the night. There's a heavenly wind got up now. It will be gorgeous riding this afternoon.'

Soon they were all on their donkeys again, jogging along round the mountain-side, enjoying the wind and the sun, gazing on the different vistas that opened up before them round every bend of the track. New mountains reared up far-away heads, new skylines appeared. For long stretches the children said nothing at all to one another, but simply drank in the beauty around them, and the sun and wind.

They travelled until six o'clock, having decided to keep to the high tea that Mrs Evans had at the farm. Jack spoke to David when six o'clock came.

'David! We stop at half-past six. Do you know a good place to camp for the night near here?'

David did not understand and Jack repeated it more slowly. David smiled and nodded.

'Iss! Iss!' This meant 'yes', and Jack looked as David pointed to a wooded spot some way ahead. David said something else in Welsh, and Jack caught a few words here and there which he understood. One was 'water', the other was 'trees'.

'David says there's a good place to camp in a little way

off!' Jack shouted back to the others. 'There's water there, and trees.'

'Gosh! However do you understand him?' said Philip in admiration. 'Jolly clever of you, Jack!'

Jack grinned all over his freckled face. 'Oh, I just caught the words "water" and "trees", that's all! Come on, let's get there in time to watch the sun sink over the mountains. I'd like to have a sunset with my sandwiches!'

Philip laughed. They all ambled on towards the spot pointed out by David. It was a little further than they thought, but when they got there they all agreed it was just the right place to camp for the night.

A spring gushed out beside the small wooded patch, as cold as ice. The trees sheltered the campers from the night-wind, which could be very chilly at times. The donkeys were to be tied to trees so that they would not wander in the night. Everything was perfect!

The children were tired but happy. They slid off their donkeys' backs, and the little beasts, tired now too, were taken to the spring to drink. They stood patiently waiting their turn, whilst Snowy skipped about like a mad thing, not in the least tired with his long trip.

'We'll put up the tents after we've had a meal and a rest,' said Philip. 'Get out the food, Lucy-Ann and Dinah. There's a nice flat stone here we can use as a table.'

Soon the supper, or high tea, was spread out on the big flat stone, and mugs of lemonade were set by each plate. The children drained them at once, and Jack was sent to get more ice-cold water from the spring.

They all ate quickly, for they were very hungry again. They said very little until the first edge of their appetite had worn off, then they all talked with their mouths full, eager to make the others remember the lovely day.

David ate too and listened. The donkeys pulled at the grass. Snowy was with Dapple, and Kiki was eating a tomato and dripping the juice down Jack's neck. They all felt as if they couldn't possibly be happier.

'Now we'll put up the tents,' said Jack at last. 'Come on, Philip! It'll be dark before we've put them up if we don't make haste!'

8

First night in camp

The girls washed the dirty crockery in the cold spring water whilst David and the boys unpacked the tents from the donkey that carried them. They took off the whole of his pack, and also unstrapped the heavy panniers from the other donkey. Both were delighted to be rid of their loads. They lay down on the ground and rolled, kicking their legs up into the air.

Kiki couldn't understand this at all, and flew up into a tree. 'She thinks they've gone mad,' said Jack. 'It's all right, Kiki, they're only feeling glad because their packs have gone!'

Kiki made a noise like a train screeching in a tunnel, and the two rolling donkeys leapt to their feet in alarm and raced some way down the hill. David also jumped violently, and then called to the donkeys.

'Kiki, if you do that again I'll tie your beak up!' threatened Jack. 'Spoiling this lovely peaceful evening with that horrible screech!'

'Wipe your feet, wipe your feet!' screamed Kiki and danced from foot to foot on her branch.

The tents were soon put up, side by side. David did not want to sleep in one. He preferred to sleep outside. He had never slept in a tent, and he thought they were quite unnecessary.

'Well, I'd just as soon he slept outside,' said Jack to Philip. 'I don't believe there'd be room for one more in here, do you?'

'Let's leave the tent-flaps open,' said Lucy-Ann, coming up with the clean crockery. 'Then we can look out down the mountain-side. I wouldn't mind a bit sleeping in the open air, like David, as a matter of fact.'

'Wind's too cold,' said Jack. 'You'll be glad to have a cosy sleeping-bag, Lucy-Ann! David must be very hardy – he's only got a thin rug to cover himself with, and he's apparently going to sleep on the bare ground!'

The sun had now disappeared completely. It had gone behind the mountains in a perfect blaze of colour, and all the summits had gleamed for a while, and then darkness had crept up to the very tops, leaving only a clear sky beyond. Stars were now winking here and there, and a cold wind was blowing up the mountain.

The donkeys were tied loosely to trees. Some of them were lying down. Dapple was looking out for Snowy, but the kid had gone to Philip, and was waiting for him to go into his tent.

They all washed at the spring – but David seemed

rather astonished to see the four children solemnly splashing themselves with the cold water. He had drawn his thin rug over him and was lying quite still, looking up to the starry sky.

'He's not what you might call a very *cheerful* companion, is he?' said Jack. 'I expect he thinks we're all quite mad, the way we joke and laugh and fool about. Buck up, Philip, and get into the tent.'

The girls were already in their tent. They had slid down into their sleeping-bags and tied them up loosely at the neck. Each bag had a big hood to come over the head. They were comfortable, quite roomy, and very warm.

Lucy-Ann could see out of the tent opening. Stars twinkled in the sky, looking very big and bright. There was no sound at all, except of the trickle-trickle of the spring, and the sound of the wind in the trees.

'We might be alone in the world,' said Lucy-Ann to Dinah. 'Dinah, imagine that we are. It gives you an awfully queer feeling. It's wizard!'

But Dinah hadn't got Lucy-Ann's imagination and she yawned. 'Go to sleep,' she said. 'Are the boys in their tent yet? I wish they were a bit further away. I've got an awful feeling that slow-worm will come slithering here in the night.'

'It won't hurt you if it does,' said Lucy-Ann, snuggling down in her sleeping-bag. 'Oh, this is super! I do think we have lovely hols, don't you, Dinah?'

But Dinah was asleep already. Her eyes had shut and she was dreaming. Lucy-Ann stayed awake a little longer, enjoying the sound of the running spring and the wind. She still felt rather as if she was on her donkey, jogging up and down. Then her eyes closed too.

The boys talked for a little while. They had thoroughly enjoyed their day. They gazed out of the open flap of the tent. 'It's pretty wild and desolate, here,' said Jack sleepily. 'It's surprising there's a track to follow, really. Decent of Bill and Aunt Allie to let us come by ourselves!'

'Mmmmmmm!' said Philip, listening, but too sleepy to answer.

'Mmmmmmm!' imitated Kiki from the top of the tent outside. It was too hot for her in it.

'There's Kiki,' said Jack. 'I wondered where she was. Philip, aren't you hot with Snowy on top of you?'

'Mmmmmmm!' said Philip, and again there came the echo from the tent-top. 'Mmmmmmm!'

Snowy was almost on top of Philip. He had tried his hardest to squeeze into the boy's sleeping-bag with him, but Philip was quite firm about that.

'If you think you're going to stick your sharp little hooves into me all night long, you're wrong, Snowy,' he said, and tied up his bag firmly at the neck, in case Snowy should try any tricks in the night. The slow-worm was somewhere about too. Philip was too sleepy to bother to think where. Sally slid about where she pleased. Philip was now quite used to the sudden slithering movement that occurred at times somewhere about his body, which meant that Sally was on the move again.

There were a few more quiet remarks from Kiki, who was apparently talking to herself. Then silence. The little camp slept under the stars. The night-wind nosed into the tent, but could not get into the cosy sleeping-bags. Snowy felt too hot, walked over Philip, trod on Jack and went to lie in the tent opening. He gave a tiny bleat and Kiki bleated in answer.

David was up and about before the children the next day. He was looking at his donkeys when Philip put a tousled head out of the tent opening to sniff at the morning. 'Lovely!' he said. 'Stop butting me, Snowy! Your little head is jolly hard! Jack! Stir yourself. It's a gorgeous morning.'

Soon all the campers were out of their sleeping-bags and running about. They splashed at the spring, laughing at nothing. Snowy bounded everywhere, quite mad too. Kiki hooted like a car, and startled the donkeys. Even David smiled to see such early-morning antics!

They had breakfast – tongue, cream cheese and rather stale bread, with a tomato each. There was no lemonade left because they had been so lavish with it the day before, so they drank the cold spring water and vowed it was just as nice as lemonade.

'David! Shall we get to the Vale of Butterflies today?' asked Jack, and then repeated it again slowly, flapping his arms to show David that he was talking about butterflies. It took David a minute or two to realize this. Then he shook his head.

'Tomorrow?' asked Philip, and David nodded. He went to strap the packs on the donkeys again and to put on the big pannier baskets. All the little grey creatures were waiting impatiently to set off. Already the sun was getting well above the mountains, and, for David and the donkeys at any rate, it was late!

They set off at last, though Jack had to gallop back to get his field-glasses which he had left behind, hanging from a tree-branch. Then they were all in a line, one donkey behind the other, ambling over the mountains with the wind in their hair.

Jack felt sure he saw a couple of buzzards that day and rode most of the time with his field-glasses in his hand, ready to clap them to his eyes at the first sight of specks in the sky. The others saw red squirrels among the trees they passed, shy but tame. One shared the children's lunch, darting up for tit-bits, but keeping a wary eye for Kiki and Snowy.

'It wants to come with you, Philip,' said Lucy-Ann, amused when the red squirrel put a paw on Philip's knee.

Philip stroked the pretty little thing gently. It quivered, half frightened, but did not bound away. Then Kiki swooped down and the squirrel fled.

'You *would* spoil things, you jealous bird!' said Philip.

'Go away, I don't want you. Go to Jack, and let the squirrels come to me.'

Swallows flew round them once again, not attracted by the food, but by the flies that pestered the donkeys. The children could hear the snapping of their beaks as they caught the flies.

'We ought to get Jack to tame a few swallows and take them with us to catch the flies,' said Lucy-Ann, slapping at a big one on her leg. 'Horrid things! I've been bitten by something already. You wouldn't think there'd be any as high up as this, would you?'

Sally the slow-worm came out to eat the fly that Lucy-Ann had killed. She was getting much too tame for Dinah's liking. She lay in the sun, gleaming like silver, and then slid under Philip as Snowy came up enquiringly.

'Keep your nose out of things,' said Philip, pushing the kid away as it tried to nose under him to find the slow-worm. Snowy butted him hard and then tried to get on his lap.

'Too hot, too hot,' said Philip. 'Why did we ever bring a little pest like you, Snowy? You breathed down my neck all night!'

Lucy-Ann giggled. She loved Snowy. They all did. The kid was mischievous, given to butting, and didn't mind treading on anyone – but he was so lively, so full of spring and bounce, so affectionate that it was impossible to be cross with him for long.

'Come on,' said Philip at last. 'David's clearing his throat as if he's going to tell us we're too lazy for words.'

David had a habit of clearing his throat about a dozen times before he spoke. It was a nervous habit which Kiki copied to perfection. She would sit near him, and make a noise as if she was clearing her throat every time he did the same thing. Then she would go off into a cackle of laughter. David always stared at her solemnly when she did this.

They travelled well that second day, and went a long way. When the time came to camp again, David looked earnestly over the mountains as if he was searching for something.

'Lost your handkerchief, old chap?' said Jack, and everyone laughed. David looked solemnly at him, not understanding. Then he suddenly began to flap his arms like wings, and to say a few words in Welsh.

He looked comical standing there, flapping like that. The children had to turn away, trying not to laugh. 'He says tomorrow we shall see the butterfly valley,' said Jack. 'Good! It ought to be a real sight, if it's anything like I imagine it to be!'

They had a meal and prepared to camp out again. The evening was not so fine as the day. It had clouded over and there was no sunset to watch, and no stars to come gleaming out, one by one.

'If it rains, you'll get wet, David,' said Jack. David shrugged his shoulders and said something in his Welsh voice, then wrapped himself in his rug on the bare ground.

'It won't rain,' said Philip, looking at the sky. 'But it's much colder. Brrrrr! I'll be glad of my sleeping-bag tonight.'

'Good night!' called the girls. 'Sleep well.'

'Good night! It will be a lovely day again tomorrow! You just see!' called back Philip, who thought himself a good weather forecaster.

But he was wrong. When they awoke the next morning, they looked out on a completely different world!

9

A different world

Lucy-Ann awoke first. She was cold. She snuggled down into her sleeping-bag, and then opened her eyes. She stared out of the open tent-flap, expecting to see the green mountain-side, and the distant mountains towering up into the sky.

But they weren't there! Instead, a white mist swirled past the tent-flap, some of it putting thin cold fingers into the tent itself.

There was nothing to see at all except this mist. The mountains had gone, the trees by the camp were blotted out, even the donkeys couldn't be seen.

'What's happened?' said Lucy-Ann, astonished. 'Golly! It's a thick mist come up!'

She awoke Dinah and the girls peered out in dismay at the misty mountain-side. Now and again a tiny bit of view could be seen as the mist thinned a little – but it grew thick again at once.

'It's a cloud,' said Dinah. 'You know how we see

clouds resting on mountain-tops – well, this is one. It's resting on *us*! It's like a thick fog we can't see through. Blow!'

The boys woke up then and the girls could hear their dismayed voices. They called to them.

'Jack! Philip! Isn't this sickening! We can't see a thing!'

'It may clear when we've had breakfast,' said Philip cheerfully, appearing out of the mist with Snowy at his heels. 'Gosh, it's chilly! I'm going to put on a warm jersey.'

David also appeared, looking very doleful. He swung his arm out towards the valley and poured out a torrent of Welsh.

'He's quite excited about it, isn't he?' said Jack. 'I wish I could follow him when he talks like that. I just don't understand a word.'

They decided to have breakfast in one of the tents because the mist made everything damp and chilly. David preferred to stay outside. Dinah didn't want to come into the tent because of Sally, and only agreed to if she was allowed to sit in the doorway, ready to escape if the slow-worm appeared.

It was not so cheerful a meal as usual. The children missed the magnificent view they had been used to, and were afraid perhaps David wouldn't take them on their way that day. But the mist cleared a little in an hour's time, and David seemed quite willing to go.

They loaded up the donkeys, mounted and set off

down the track. They could see some way ahead of them now, for the sun was rising higher, and trying to dissolve the mist with its heat.

'It'll be all right,' said Jack. 'I *almost* caught sight of the sun then!'

But then the mist came down again and it was only just possible to see the donkey in front.

'I feel as if I ought to hold your donkey's tail, in case you disappear in the mist!' shouted Jack to Dinah. 'You know – like elephants do in circuses when they come into the ring all holding on to one another's tails!'

The mist thickened even more, and the little company stopped to discuss what to do. It was difficult to get anything intelligible out of David, who seemed suddenly to have forgotten any English words he knew.

Jack flapped his arms, raised his eyebrows and pointed in front of him, meaning to ask if they were near the Butterfly Valley. David understood, but he hesitated.

'I hope he hasn't lost the way,' said Jack to Philip. 'He seemed sure enough of the direction yesterday – now he doesn't seem very certain. Blow!'

'Well, we can't stop here,' said Dinah, shivering in the clammy mist. 'There's no shelter and it's jolly cold. Oh for the sun again!'

'Ride on!' said Jack to David. 'It's the only thing to do till we find some kind of shelter. It's too cold to hang about till the mist has gone. If we go the wrong way we can turn back and go right when the mist goes.'

So they went on, following David's donkey through the wet mist. Kiki was very silent. She didn't understand the mist and was afraid of it. Snowy kept close to Philip's donkey, and was not nearly so full of spring and liveliness. Everyone disliked the mist thoroughly.

'When we find a sheltered place we'll stop for lunch,' said Philip. 'I'm sure we're all getting frightfully hungry now, but we seem to be on quite a bare bit of mountainside, hopeless to picnic in. We'd all be down with colds tomorrow!'

They ambled on, nose to tail, pulling their jerseys close, glad of their coats too. Jack began to look rather worried. He stopped his donkey and went to walk beside Philip's.

'What's up?' said Philip, seeing Jack's serious face.

'We've left the track,' said Jack. 'Haven't you noticed? We've followed some kind of track up till an hour or two back – but now I'm pretty certain we've lost it. Goodness knows where David's heading for. I doubt if he's even noticed we're not on any track at all.'

Philip whistled. 'Don't let the girls hear you. They'll be scared. Yes, you're right. There's not the vestige of a track here. David's lost the way.'

'Better ask him,' said Jack and rode to the front of the line. 'Is this the right way?' he asked David slowly, so as to be understood. 'Where is the track?' He pointed downwards to the ground.

David was looking solemn too. He shrugged his

shoulders and said something in his sing-song voice. Jack rode back to Philip.

'I think he knows he's off the track, but he's hoping to pick it up further on. Anyway he doesn't seem inclined to stop or go back.'

'Well – he's our guide,' said Philip, after a pause. 'We'll have to trust him. He knows these mountains better than we do.'

'Yes. But he's so shy,' said Jack. 'He wouldn't be able to tell us we were lost. I wouldn't put it past him to go on losing us deeper and deeper in these mountains, once he'd begun! He just wouldn't know what else to do.'

'What a horrible idea!' said Philip. 'Good thing we've got so much food with us, if that's what he means to do!'

They came at last to a big outcrop of rocks, which would give them shelter from the wet, chilly wind. 'Better have a meal here,' said Philip. 'I'd like something hot to drink. Did Mrs Evans put in a kettle?'

'Yes. If we can find a stream or spring, we'll build a little fire and boil some water for cocoa or something,' said Jack.

But there was no spring and no stream. It was most annoying.

'Considering the *dozens* we've passed this morning, and waded through, I call it a bit hard that there's not even a tiny one here,' said Dinah. 'I'm jolly thirsty too.'

They had to have a meal without anything to drink. They were very hungry, and the food seemed to warm them a little. They played a game of Catch to get them-selves thoroughly warm after the meal. David looked as if he thought they had gone mad. Snowy joined in wildly, neatly tripping everyone up. Kiki rose in the air and screamed.

'Look at David's face! He thinks we're all crazy!' giggled Lucy-Ann. She sank down on a rock. 'Oh, I can't run any more. I've got a stitch in my side.'

'Stitchinmyside, stitchinmyside,' chanted Kiki, run-ning all the words together. 'Pop goes the weasel!'

'The mist's clearing! Hurrah!' suddenly cried Jack, and he pointed upwards. The sun could quite clearly be seen, struggling to get through the clouds of mist.

Everyone cheered up at once. Even David looked less dismal. 'Let's try to get to the Butterfly Valley before the evening,' said Jack to David, doing the flapping business vigorously to make sure David understood. David nodded.

They mounted the donkeys again and set off once more. They could see much further in front of them now. Quite a big stretch of mountain-side was spread before them. The world suddenly seemed a much bigger place.

They rode on steadily. The mist thinned more and more rapidly, and the children felt the heat of the sun on their heads. They took off their coats, revelling in the warmth, after the chilliness of the mist.

'Look – we can see the nearest mountain-tops now,'

called Jack. 'And the distant ones will soon be uncovered too. Thank goodness!'

'We ought to see the Vale of Butterflies soon,' said Lucy-Ann, eagerly. 'David said we'd get there today. I wonder where it is. Look, there's a butterfly, Philip.'

Philip glanced at it. 'Only a meadow-brown,' he said. 'We've seen heaps of those.' He looked before him searchingly and then put his field-glasses to his eyes.

'There's a valley which *might* be it,' he said, pointing. 'Hey, David! Is that the Vale of Butterflies?'

David looked where Philip was pointing. He shrugged his shoulders. 'Iss. No,' he said.

'Yes, no! Whatever does he mean by that?' said Philip in disgust. 'I suppose, in plain English, he means he hasn't the faintest idea. Well, we'll go on and hope for the best. It looks a nice sheltered kind of valley, the sort that might be hot enough for all kinds of insects and flowers.'

Picturing a perfect paradise of brilliant flowers and equally brilliant butterflies, the children rode on and on down towards the valley in the far distance. It was much further than they thought. That was the worst of travelling in mountains. Everywhere was about twice as far as you imagined it to be. Most disappointing!

It was late when they rode into the valley, which was really more of a shallow depression between two high mountains than a real lowland valley. Certainly it was sheltered, and certainly it had more flowers in it than they had so far seen – but there were no butterflies!

'This can't be it!' said Philip in disappointment. 'Is it, David?'

David shook his head. He was looking round in a puzzled manner, and it was quite clear that he really didn't know where he was.

'If this is *not* the butterfly place, where is it?' asked Jack slowly and clearly. David shook his head again. It was really maddening, not being able to speak Welsh.

'Well,' said Philip, 'he's brought us the wrong way, to a place he doesn't know, but it's quite warm and sheltered, so we'll make the best of it tonight. Tomorrow we'll get the map from David, see if *we* can find out the way, and set off with ourselves as guides. He's as much use as Kiki to guide us in these mountains!'

They set up their camp again, feeling rather disappointed. They had so hoped to come to the place they wanted that night, and set up camp properly for a few days, to revel in hordes of common and uncommon butterflies. Now they would have to ride on still further, and goodness knew if they would ever find it!

They crawled into their sleeping-bags and called good night, just as the stars gleamed out. David was sleeping as usual outside.

But in the night the boys woke up suddenly. David was crawling into their tent. He was trembling with fright. 'Noises,' he said, in English, and then poured out something in Welsh. He was very frightened. 'Sleep here,' he said, and crept between the boys. They were amused and puzzled.

Whatever *could* have scared David so much?

10

A disturbing night

The sun was shining brightly when the camp awoke next day. It made them all feel cheerful and lively. Snowy, who had resented David sleeping with Philip and Jack the night before, and had butted him continually, bounded about lightly everywhere, butting David whenever he met him.

'What happened to you last night, David?' asked Jack, when they were all having a meal. 'Why were you so frightened?'

'Noises,' said David.

'What sort?' asked Philip curiously. '*We* didn't hear any.'

David made some surprising noises that sent Kiki sailing into the air and Snowy bounding away in fright. The children stared at David in astonishment.

By means of odd words and gestures David managed to convey to the children that he had gone to see if the donkeys were all right in the night, and had heard these noises near by where they were tethered.

'That explains why *we* didn't hear them, I suppose,' said Jack. 'David makes them sound like animal noises – fierce and savage!'

Lucy-Ann looked scared. 'Oh! You don't think there are wild animals anywhere about here, do you, Jack? I mean, *fierce* wild animals?'

Jack grinned. 'Well, if you are thinking of lions and tigers and panthers and bears, I think I can say you needn't be afraid of finding *those* here. But if, like Dinah, you include snakes, foxes, hedgehogs and so on in your list of fierce wild animals, then I should say, look out!'

'Don't be silly, Jack. Of course I don't mean those,' said Lucy-Ann. 'I don't quite know what I *did* mean. I just felt scared – and wondered what animal had made the noises David heard.'

'Probably his own imagination,' said Philip. 'Or a bad dream. That could scare him.'

David did not seem to want to go any further. He kept pointing back over the way they had come. But the children were not going to let their trip come to such a disappointing end. They meant to go and find the Butterfly Valley, if it took them all week! There was a lot of flapping to make David understand this.

He turned even more silent, but mounted his donkey to go with them. Jack now had the map, and examined it very carefully. It was annoying that the Butterfly Valley wasn't marked. Perhaps very few people knew about it.

They all set off across the valley and up into the mountains again. Perhaps the next valley would be the one they wanted, or the one after that. But although they travelled hopefully all the day, they did not find any valley full of butterflies. The children began to think it was all a fairy-tale.

There was no track to follow now, though they kept a keen look-out in case they should come across one again. When they camped that night, they discussed what they had better do next.

'If we go on any further we shan't know our way back,' said Jack. 'David would, perhaps, because he was born and bred among mountains, and, like a dog, could follow his own trail well enough, if we had to go back. But he's lost us once and I don't like to trust him too much. I wouldn't be surprised if he lost the way going back, if we take him much further!'

'Had we better go back then?' asked Lucy-Ann in disappointment.

'Or camp here for a few days,' said Jack, looking round. 'It's quite a good place.'

They were halfway up a steep mountain that rose very sharply from where they were, and looked quite unclimbable.

'What a peculiar mountain!' said Dinah, gazing up. 'I

shouldn't think anyone ever climbed that to the top. It's all crags and rocks and jutting-out bits.'

'We'll camp here,' decided Philip. 'The weather looks quite settled. There's a spring near by. We can mess about with our cameras and field-glasses.'

They told David. He did not seem pleased, but went off to tether the donkeys for the night. They were all tired that evening, children and donkeys both, for they had had a very long day. They cut the big ham that Mrs Evans had provided for them, afraid that it might go bad if they didn't eat it soon.

David looked as if he thought he would sleep in the tent again that night, for he cast various longing glances in that direction. However, the night was hot, and he felt he couldn't bear to be under cover. So he arranged himself under his rug in the open, fairly near to the two tents. The donkeys were some way away, tethered to trees by long ropes.

That night there was a snuffling around the camp. Lucy-Ann awoke suddenly and heard it. She went right down to the bottom of her sleeping-bag, frightened. What could it be? Was it the wild animal that David had heard?

Then she heard a howl! The boys heard it too, and awoke. David, outside, was awake, having heard both the noises. He was shivering with fright, all kinds of fears coming into his mind at once.

The moon was up and everywhere was silvery bright.

David sat up and looked down the hill. What he saw made his hair rise straight up on his head.

Wolves! A pack of wolves! No, no, it couldn't be wolves! He was dreaming! Wolves had not been known in the mountains for hundreds of years. But if those creatures were not wolves, what were they? And that noise of snuffling he had heard. That must have been a wolf too! No, not a *wolf*. It couldn't have been such a thing.

David sat there, hugging his knees, his mind going round and round – wolves or not? Wolves or not? What were they doing near the donkeys?

Another howl came – half a howl, half a bark, a horrible noise. David shot into the boys' tent and gave them a terrible start.

He stammered something in Welsh, and then in English, 'Wolves!'

'Don't be silly,' said Jack at once, seeing that the man was badly scared. 'You've had a bad dream.'

David dragged him to the tent opening and pointed with a trembling finger to where the pack of snuffling animals stood, not far from the donkeys.

The boys stared as if they could not believe their eyes. They certainly *looked* like wolves! Jack felt a cold shiver down his back. Good gracious! Was he dreaming? Those creatures were more like wolves than anything else!

Snowy the kid was trembling as much as David was. The trembling somehow made the boys feel scared too.

The only person who was not in the least scared was Kiki.

She too had caught sight of the wolves. She sailed out of the tent at top speed to go and investigate. Anything unusual always interested Kiki. She flew above the animals, whose eyes gleamed green as they turned at her coming.

'Wipe your feet!' screamed Kiki, and made a noise like a mowing-machine cutting long grass. It sounded really terrible in the still night air of the mountain-side.

The wolves started in fright. Then with one accord they all galloped away down the hillside into the night. Kiki shouted rude remarks after them.

'They've gone,' said Jack. 'Gosh, were they real? I can't understand it!'

When it was dawn, David got up to see if the donkeys were all right. Neither he nor the boys had slept again that night. David had been too scared to, and the boys had been too puzzled.

Daylight was almost on the mountain. David crept down quietly to the donkeys. They were all there, safe and sound but uneasy. David untethered them to take them to the stream to drink.

The boys were looking out of their tent, down the hillside to watch. There was no sign of any wolf now. Birds sang a little, and a yellow-hammer cried out for a little bit of bread and no cheese.

Suddenly something happened. David, who was

taking the donkeys in a line to the stream, gave a terrified yell and fell to the ground, covering his face. The boys, holding their breath, thought they saw something moving in the bushes, but they couldn't see what.

David gave another yell and got to his feet. He mounted a donkey and rode at top speed up to the tent.

'Come!' he cried in Welsh, and then in English. 'Black, black, black!'

The boys had no idea at all what he meant. They stared at him in amazement, thinking he must have gone mad. He made a violent gesture to them, pointed to the following donkeys as if to tell the boys to mount and follow him, and then galloped off at breakneck speed.

They heard the hooves of his donkey echoing on the mountain-side for some time. The other donkeys looked doubtfully at one another, and then, to the boys' dismay, trotted after David!

'Hi! Come back, David!' yelled Jack, scrambling out of the tent. 'Hi, hi!'

One donkey turned and made as if to come back, but he was pushed on by the others behind. In a trice they had all disappeared, and the sound of their hooves grew fainter and fainter as they galloped away after David and his mount.

The two boys sat down suddenly. They felt faint. Jack turned pale. He looked at Philip and bit his lip. Now they were in a terrible fix.

They said nothing for a moment or two, and then the girls' two scared faces looked out from their tent.

'What's happened? What's all the yelling? Was that David galloping away? We didn't dare to look!'

'Yes – it was David – running away from us – and all the donkeys have gone after him,' said Philip bitterly. 'We're in a pretty fix now!'

Nobody said anything. Lucy-Ann looked really alarmed. No David! No donkeys! What were they going to do?

Jack put his arm round her as she came and sat down beside him. 'It's all right! We've been in worse fixes than this! At the worst it only means a few days here, because as soon as he gets back to the farm, Bill will come and look for us.'

'Good thing we unloaded the donkeys and have got plenty of food,' said Philip. 'And our tents and sleeping-bags. Blow David! He's a nuisance.'

'I wonder what he saw to make him gallop off like that,' said Jack. 'All I could make out was "Black, black, black!"'

'Black what?' asked Dinah.

'Black nothing. Just black,' said Jack. 'Let's go down to the place where he got his fright and see if we can see anything.'

'Oh *no*!' said the girls at once.

'Well, I'll go, and Philip can stay here with you,' said Jack, and off he went. The others watched him, holding their breath. He peered all round and then turned and shook his head and shouted.

'Nothing here! Not a thing to see! David must have been seeing things! His bad night upset him.'

He came back. 'But what about those animals in the night?' said Philip, after a pause. 'Those wolves. We both saw those. *They* seemed real enough!'

Yes – what about those wolves!

11

A strange happening

It wasn't long before Dinah suggested having something to eat, and went to the big panniers that had been unloaded from the donkeys the night before. She pulled out some tins, thinking it would be a change to have sardines, and tinned peaches, or something like that. Anything to take their minds off David's flight, and the disappearance of the donkeys!

They sat down rather silently. Lucy-Ann kept very close to the boys. What with wolves and David's fright she felt very scared herself!

'I hope this won't turn into one of our adventures,' she kept saying to herself. 'They always happen so suddenly.'

Snowy the kid bounded up to Philip and knocked a tin flying from his hand. He nuzzled affectionately against him and then butted him. Philip rubbed the furry little nose and then pushed the kid away.

'I'm glad *you* didn't go off with the donkeys too!' he

said. 'I've got used to having you around now, you funny aggravating little thing. Take your nose out of that tin! Lucy-Ann, push him off – he'll eat everything we've got!'

Kiki suddenly flew at Snowy, screaming with rage. She had had her eye on that tin of sliced peaches, and to see Snowy nosing round it was too much for her. She gave him a sharp peck on the nose, and he ran to Philip, bleating. Everyone laughed and felt better.

They sat there, eating by the tents, occasionally glancing up at the mountain that towered up so steeply above them. It had no gentle slope up to the summit, as most of the mountains around had, but was steep and forbidding.

'I don't much like this mountain,' said Lucy-Ann.

'Why?' asked Dinah.

'I don't know. I just don't like it,' said Lucy-Ann. 'I've got one of my "feelings" about it.'

The others laughed. Lucy-Ann often had 'feelings' about things, and really believed in them. It was just like her to start having 'feelings' about the mountain, when everyone was also having uncomfortable ideas about wolves and other things.

'Well, you needn't have any "feelings" about mountains,' said Philip. 'Mountains are all the same – just tops, middles and bottoms, sometimes with sheep on and sometimes without!'

'But not many have wolves,' said Lucy-Ann seriously, and that made the others feel uncomfortable again.

'What are we going to do today?' asked Jack, when they had finished their meal. 'I suppose we *must* stay here till Bill comes to find us. We can't try to walk back home, because for one thing we don't know the way, and for another we'd never be able to carry enough food to get there without starving.'

'We'd far better stay here,' said Philip at once. 'It's ten chances to one David will know his way back here all right, and can bring Bill and the donkeys. Whereas if we start moving about, they'll never find us.'

'Yes – it does seem the most sensible thing to do,' said Jack. 'We've got our camp here – tents set up and everything – so we might as well make the best of it, and enjoy the camping. I wish there was somewhere to bathe though. It's so jolly hot. That little stream's too small to do anything but paddle in.'

'Let's all keep together,' said Lucy-Ann. 'I mean – we could frighten those wolves away perhaps if we all screamed at them – but one of us alone might be – might be . . .'

'Gobbled up!' said Jack, and laughed. 'What big *eyes* you've got, Granny! And, oh, what big TEETH you've got!'

'Don't tease her,' said Philip, seeing Lucy-Ann's alarmed face. 'It's all right, Lucy-Ann. Wolves are only really hungry in the winter-time and it's summer now.'

Lucy-Ann looked relieved. 'Well – I suppose if they'd been really hungry they would have attacked the donkeys, wouldn't they?' she said. 'Oh dear – I do think it's most extraordinary to find wolves here.'

They were just about to get up and clear away the picnic things when something curious happened that froze them to the ground.

First of all there was a grumbling, rumbling noise that seemed to come from the heart of the mountain itself – and then the ground shook a little. The four children distinctly felt it quivering beneath them, and they clutched at one another in alarm. Kiki flew straight up into the air, screaming. Snowy leapt to a high rock and stood there, poised on his four little legs as if to take off in the air like a plane.

The ground stopped shaking. The noise died away. But almost imediately the rumbling began again, a little louder, but very muffled as if great depths of rock separated it from the listeners. The ground quivered once more and Snowy took a flying leap into the air, landing on another rock. He was really terrified.

So were the four children. Lucy-Ann, very pale, clung to Jack and Philip. Dinah, forgetting all about the slow-worm, held on to Philip too.

There were no more rumblings, and the earth beneath them stayed still. The birds, which had stopped singing and calling, began to chirp again, and a yellow-hammer gave his familiar cry.

Snowy recovered himself and came bounding up to

the others. Kiki landed on Jack's shoulder. 'God save the Queen,' she said, in a relieved voice.

'What in the *world* was that?' said Philip at last. 'An earthquake? Gosh, I *was* scared!'

'Oh, Philip! This mountain isn't a volcano, is it?' said Lucy-Ann, gazing up at it fearfully.

'Of course not! You'd know a volcano all right if you saw one!' said Jack. 'This is a perfectly ordinary mountain – and goodness knows why it should have rumbled like that, and trembled beneath us. It gave me a horrible feeling.'

'I told you I had one of my "feelings" about this mountain,' said Lucy-Ann. 'Didn't I? I feel very peculiar about it. I want to go back to the farmhouse and not stay here.'

'So do we all,' said Philip. 'But we shouldn't know the way, Lucy-Ann. It isn't as if we'd followed a track – we left the track as you know, and part of the way we were in thick mist – we shouldn't have the faintest idea of the way.'

'I know you're right,' said Lucy-Ann. 'But I *don't* like this mountain – especially when it starts to rumble and shake! What made it?'

Nobody knew. They got up, cleared away the meal and went to splash in the little stream. The wind suddenly began to blow rather chilly, and, looking up, the children saw that big clouds were coming up from the south-west.

'Looks like rain,' said Jack. I hope the wind doesn't get up much more, or it will blow our tents away. Do you remember how they were blown clean away from over us on our last adventure – on the Island of Birds? That was an awful feeling.'

'Well,' said Philip, 'if you really think the tents might blow away, Jack, we'd better find a better place to camp than this – somewhere not too far, though, because we don't want to miss seeing Bill and David when they come for us. A copse of trees or a cave or somewhere like that – right out of the wind.'

'Let's look now,' said Dinah, pulling on her coat. It was extraordinary how cold it got as soon as the sun went in and the wind blew up the mountain. 'We'd better take Snowy with us, or he'll eat everything we've left!'

Snowy had every intention of coming with them. He capered along by Philip and Jack, as mad as ever. He was now very annoyed with Kiki, and leapt at her whenever she came within reach, wanting to pay her back for nipping his nose.

When the girls had been left a little way behind, Philip spoke in a low voice to Jack. 'We'd better find a cave, I think, Jack – I don't like the idea of those animals prowling around us at night – wolves, or whatever they are. If we were in a cave we could light a fire at the entrance and that would keep any animal off.'

'Yes. That's quite a good idea,' agreed Jack. 'I hadn't thought of that. I can't say *I* like the idea either of wolves nosing round our tents when we're asleep at night! I'd feel much safer in a cave!'

They hunted about for some kind of rocky shelter or cave, but there seemed none to be found. The mountain was so steep that it really was difficult to climb, and Lucy-Ann was afraid of slipping and falling.

Snowy leapt ahead of them, as sure-footed as ever. The boys wished heartily that it was as easy for them to leap about the mountain as it was for the kid.

'Look at him up there, standing on that rock!' said Jack, feeling exasperated and far too hot with his climbing. 'Hey, Snowy, come and give us a leg up! If only we had four springy legs like yours!'

Snowy stood there, whisking his little tail, and then ran back and disappeared. 'Where's he gone?' said Jack. 'Oh, there he comes again. Philip, there must be a cave or overhanging rock up where he is – he keeps going back and disappearing into it, whatever it is!'

They climbed up to where Snowy was, and sure enough, just at the back of the overhanging rock was a long low cave, its roof made out of another overhanging rock, its opening fringed with ferns of all kinds.

'This would do awfully well for us,' said Jack, going down on hands and knees and looking in. 'We could light a fire on the rock outside – the one Snowy stood on – and feel quite safe tonight. Clever little Snowy! You found us just what we wanted!'

'But how in the world are we going to get everything

up here?' said Philip. 'It was such a climb. It's not as if we are donkeys or goats, able to scramble up steep places quite easily, even with a load to carry. We need our hands to help us.'

This was certainly a problem. The boys hailed the girls and helped them up on to the rock where Snowy stood. 'Look,' said Jack, 'here's a good place to sleep in tonight. We can quite well see from here if Bill and David come – see what a good view we have from this rock – and we'd be safe from the wolves if we lighted a fire at the entrance to the cave.'

'Oh, *yes*!' said Lucy-Ann, pleased. She went into the cave. She had to bend her head at the opening, but inside the roof grew higher. 'It's not *really* a cave!' she said. 'It's just a space under that big jutting-out rock – but it will do awfully well.'

They all sat down on the rock, wishing the sun would come out. Snowy lay down beside them and Kiki sat on Jack's shoulder.

But suddenly she rose up into the air and screeched loudly. Snowy leapt up and stood looking downwards. What was the matter?

'Is it the wolves again?' asked Lucy-Ann in alarm. They listened. They could hear a noise of some animal or animals down below in the thick bushes, under the birch-trees.

'Get back into the cave,' said Jack to the girls. 'And keep quiet.'

The two girls went silently back into the darkness of the cave. The boys listened and watched. What animal was it down there? It must be big, by the noise it made!

12

Wolves in the night!

Snowy suddenly bleated loudly and took a flying leap off the rock before Philip could stop him. He disappeared into the bushes below – and then a loud and welcome sound filled the air.

'Ee-ore! Ee-ore! Ee-ore!'

'Goodness! It's a donkey!' cried Jack and scrambled down to see. 'Have they come back? Is David with them?'

They soon found what they were looking for. Dapple the donkey was in the bushes, nuzzling Snowy, evidently full of delight at seeing him again. But there was no sign at all of the other donkeys or of David.

'Dapple! You darling!' said Lucy-Ann, running up to him in joy. 'You've come back to us.'

'Come back to *Snowy*, you mean!' said Philip. 'He was always fond of Snowy, weren't you, Dapple? So you came back to find him. Well, we're very very glad to see you, because you will solve a very knotty problem for us – how to get all our goods up to that cave!'

Dapple *had* come back to see Snowy, but he was also very pleased to see the children again. He was a quiet, stout little donkey, hard-working and patient. He kept close to the children, and had evidently made up his mind he was going to stay with them. Snowy was sweet with him, and trotted by his side all the time.

'Here, Dapple!' called Philip. 'Come and help us with these things, there's a good fellow.'

Dapple stood obediently whilst the boys strapped things on to his back. He took all the bedding up to the cave first, scrambling up the steep bits with difficulty, but managing very well indeed. Then he took up the panniers of food.

'Thanks, Dapple,' said Jack, giving him a pat. 'Now come and have a drink!'

They all went to the stream and drank and splashed. The sun had come out again and immediately it was very hot. The children flung off their coats and lay about, basking.

'We must collect wood for the fire tonight,' said Jack. 'We shall need a good lot if we're going to keep the fire going all night long. We'll stack it in the big panniers and get Dapple to take it up for us.'

'Good old Dapple!' said Dinah.

They collected as much wood as they could, and soon it was all piled up on the rock outside the cave. The boys made a fire but did not light it. There was no need to do that till night.

The day soon went, and the sun sank behind the mountains in a blaze of crimson. As soon as darkness fell on the mountain-side, the children retired into the cave. The thought of wolves kept coming into their minds, and David's scream of terror, when he had seen something in the bushes, 'Black, black, black!' What *could* he have seen?

The children hadn't thought much of these things during the bright daylight, but they came back into their minds now it was dark. They debated whether or not to have Dapple in the cave with them.

But Dapple settled that idea by firmly refusing to go under the overhanging rock. He just stood outside stubbornly, his four legs set firmly on the ground, and no amount of pushing or pulling made the slightest difference. He was *not* going into that cave!

'All right, Dapple,' said Jack crossly. 'Stay outside and be eaten by wolves if you want to!'

'Oh, *don't* say things like that,' said Lucy-Ann. 'Dapple, do come inside! Please!'

Dapple lay down firmly outside, and the children gave it up. There would be no difficulty about Snowy or Kiki. One would want to be with Philip, the other with Jack.

'Now we'll light the fire,' said Jack, as stars began to

glimmer in the sky. 'It's getting very dark. Got the matches, Philip?'

The fire soon burnt up, for the twigs and branches were very dry. The cheerful flames leapt and flickered, and the fire crackled merrily.

'That's very very nice,' said Lucy-Ann, pleased. 'I feel safe tucked away in this cave with a fire at the entrance. Philip, make Snowy go the other side of you. He's sticking his hooves into me. I wish he'd wear bedroom slippers at night!'

Everybody laughed. They all felt safe and comfortable, tucked up in their sleeping-bags, with the fire lighting up the cave, filling it with jumping shadows. Snowy was pressed against Philip, Kiki was on Jack's middle. Somewhere outside was Dapple. Lucy-Ann wished he was in with them, then the whole family would be safe.

They all watched the flames for a while and then fell asleep. The fire flickered down as the wood was burnt up, and soon only the embers glowed.

Philip woke up with a start a few hours later. He saw that the fire had died down, and he got out of his sleeping-bag to put on more wood. It would never do to let it go out!

Dapple was still outside, lying quietly. Philip saw him when the flames leapt up to burn the wood he piled on. The boy went back to his sleeping-bag. He found that

Snowy had crept inside it whilst he was piling wood on the fire.

'You little scamp!' he whispered. 'Get out. There's not room for us both.'

There was quite a scuffle as he tried to get Snowy out of the bag. Fortunately the others were so very sound asleep that they didn't wake. Philip got Snowy out at last and slid in himself. He hastily laced up the neck of the bag before Snowy could try to squeeze in again. Snowy gave a sigh and lay down heavily right on Philip's middle.

Philip lay awake, watching the fire. The wind sometimes blew the smoke towards the cave, and for a moment or two the smell made Philip want to cough.

Then he heard Dapple stir outside, and he got up on one elbow to see why. His heart began to beat very fast.

Silent dark figures were slinking up to the cave! They did not pass beyond the fire, but they did not seem to be afraid of it. Philip felt breathless, and his heart beat even faster, as if he had been running.

What were those figures? Were they the wolves? The boy caught sight of two gleaming eyes, shining like the headlights of a distant car – but green as grass! He sat up quietly.

The wolves were back! They had smelt out the little company. What would they do? They had not attacked Dapple, thank goodness – and the donkey did not seem to be unduly frightened. He was only moving uneasily.

The slinking figures moved to and fro behind the fire.

Philip couldn't think what in the world to do! He could only hope that the fire would frighten them enough to keep them out of the cave.

After a while all the animals disappeared. Philip breathed again! Gosh, what a horrible fright he had had! What a blessing they had thought of that fire! Philip made up his mind that he wasn't going to sleep again that night, in case the fire went out. At all costs he must keep that up.

So the boy lay wide-eyed, thinking of wolves, rumblings, earthquakes and 'Black, black, black'. There was something very unusual about all these things. Did they fit together, or didn't they? *Was* there something peculiar about this mountain?

The fire was dying down again. Philip got up cautiously to put more wood on. The moon was up now and he could see for miles. He piled wood on the fire and the flames shot up. He slipped out of the cave to Dapple.

Then the boy heard a sound. He looked up – and to his horror he saw a wolf between him and the cave! He had gone to pat Dapple – and in that moment the wolf had slunk in between fire and cave. Would he go in?

The wolf stood still, looking at Philip in the moonlight. Philip gazed back, wondering what to do if the creature attacked him – and as he looked, a very peculiar thing happened.

The wolf wagged its long tail! To and fro it went, to and fro, like a big dog's! Philip's heart leapt. The animal wanted to be friendly! All animals were attracted to Philip – but a wolf! That was extraordinary.

The boy held out his hand, half afraid, but bold and daring. The wolf trotted round the fire and licked Philip's hand. It gave a little whine.

The moon shone down brightly on the animal's dark coat, pointed ears and long muzzle. *Was* it a wolf? Now that he was close to it Philip began to doubt.

And then quite suddenly he knew what this friendly animal was!

'Why, you're an Alsatian *dog*!' he cried. 'Aren't you? Why didn't I think of it before? I *knew* there weren't wolves in this country! Where are the others? You're all Alsatians! Good dog! Fine dog! I'd like to be friends with you!'

The big Alsatian put his paws up on Philip's shoulders and licked his face. Then he lifted his head and howled. It was a wolf-like noise, but Philip no longer minded that!

It was a call to the other dogs, the rest of the pack. There came the sound of feet in the bushes below, and a crowd of dogs leapt up on to the rock. They clustered round Philip, and, seeing that their leader was so friendly with the boy, they pawed him and licked him.

The howl awakened all the three children in the cave, and they sat up in fright. To their unspeakable horror they saw, outside the cave, what looked like Philip being attacked by wolves!

'Look! They've got Philip! Quick!' yelled Jack.

All three children slid out of their sleeping-bags and rushed to Philip's aid. The dogs growled at the sudden commotion.

'Philip! We're coming! Are you hurt?' cried valiant little Lucy-Ann, picking up a stick.

'It's all right, it's all right!' yelled Philip. 'They're not attacking me. They're friendly. They're not wolves, but Alsatians! Dogs, you know!'

'Goodness gracious!' said Dinah, and came out into the moonlight, so glad that the dogs were not wolves that she didn't even feel afraid of so many big dogs!

'Oh, Philip!' said Lucy-Ann, almost in tears with the shock of delight at knowing the wolves were only dogs. 'Oh, Philip! I thought you were being attacked.'

'You were a darling to come to my rescue then,' said Philip, smiling when he saw the little stick that Lucy-Ann had meant to attack the wolves with. 'The leader of the dogs made friends with me – so all the others are doing the same!'

The dogs had apparently made up their minds to stay for the night. Philip debated what to do. 'We can't possibly go back into the cave,' he said. 'The whole pack will come crowding in, and it would be impossible to breathe.'

'Quite impossible,' said Dinah, filled with horror at the thought of so many dogs sleeping with them.

'So we'll bring our sleeping-bags out here on the rock

beside Dapple, and sleep there,' said Philip. 'The dogs can stay if they want to – they'll be good guards! And if they don't want to, they can go. There are about ten of them! I wonder how it is they're wandering about here wild. Ten of them! It's extraordinary.'

They dragged out their sleeping-bags, and got into them. The dogs sniffed round in wonder. The leader sat majestically down by Philip, as if to say, 'This boy is my property. Keep off!' The others lay about among the children. Snowy was afraid of the big leader-dog and dared not even go near his beloved Philip. He went to Jack instead. Kiki stayed up in a tree. There were altogether too many dogs for her!

It was a curious sight the moon looked down on: four children, one goat, one parrot, one donkey – and ten dogs!

13

The face in the tree

When the morning came, Dapple awoke the children by giving a mighty sneeze. They woke with a jump, wondering what it was. Dapple gave another sneeze, and they knew!

'It's Dapple! Have you got a cold, Dapple?' asked Lucy-Ann anxiously. Then she remembered the happenings of the night, and looked round.

Everyone said the same thing at once.

'Where are the dogs?'

They had disappeared. Not one was there. The children looked at one another, puzzled. Where had they gone, and why?

'We couldn't *all* have dreamed them,' said Dinah, answering everyone's unspoken thought. 'They really were here. Ten of them. Most peculiar.'

'Yes, it *is* peculiar,' said Jack. 'Personally, I think they must belong to somebody. They didn't strike me as being a pack of *wild* dogs.'

'Nor me,' said Philip. 'But who could they belong to? There's not a house for miles! And why should anyone in this desolate mountain country keep ten man-hunting dogs?'

'Oooh – are they man-hunters?' said Lucy-Ann, startled.

'Well, the police use them for that,' said Philip. 'Don't they, Jack? They hunt criminals with them. Those Alsatians can smell them out and capture them. But there can't be any police here, with hunting-dogs! I mean – Bill would have had it reported to him, if they were. He's high up in the police organization himself, and there's not a thing he doesn't know about what's going on in the police world.'

'Where do the dogs come from then?' asked Dinah. 'Would they be kept as guards for anything – to frighten anyone off, or give the alarm, for instance?'

'Yes – but what is there to guard here, among these mountains?' said Jack. 'Nothing at all, as far as I can see!'

'Give it up!' said Philip, sliding out of his sleeping-bag. 'I'm going for a splash in the stream. Coming?'

'Yes. Then we'll open a tin or two,' said Dinah. 'I wish we'd thought of giving that ham-bone to the dogs, Jack. The ham's gone bad now – but they wouldn't have minded.'

'We'll give it to them next time we see them,' said Jack. 'I've no doubt they'll be along again!'

They all splashed in the stream, Snowy and Dapple

too. Kiki sat apart, making sarcastic remarks, for she was not fond of water.

'Pooh! Gah!' she shouted, trying to remember all the rude words she knew. 'Gooh! Pah!'

'That's right. Mix your words up, Kiki,' said Jack. 'What about "piffle" and "bunk"? You used to know those too.'

'Pifflebunk,' said Kiki, and thought that was a good word. 'Pifflebunk, bifflebunk, pop goes the pifflebunk.'

The children laughed. Kiki laughed too and then began to give an imitation of Dapple braying. This was much too lifelike and Dapple started up, looking all round for the other donkeys.

'Ee-ore, ee-ore, ee-ore,' went on Kiki, till Jack threw a towel at her to make her stop. It fell over her head and she screamed in rage. Dapple and Snowy stared solemnly at her, puzzled and surprised.

They had a meal. Lucy-Ann volunteered to go down to the stream again and wash the dishes, whilst the others looked at the map, trying to find out exactly where they were. She went off to the stream, humming.

She knelt down by the water, scouring a dish, when a sound made her look up. She had heard something in the tree above, just by the water.

There was a big, leafy tree there, growing almost out of the stream. Lucy-Ann, thinking there must be a bird in the tree, peered up into the branches.

She got a terrible shock. Looking down at her was a face – and it was black.

The little girl sat there, petrified, the dish in her hand, unable to move or speak. The branches moved and she saw that the face was topped by black, thick hair, and had bright eyes and a cheerful expression.

'It's a black man!' she thought to herself. 'But here! Up this tree! What shall I do?'

The black face looked down on the little girl, and then the man's lips parted in a smile. The head nodded amiably. Then a black finger came up from among the leaves, and was put to the lips.

'Don't you make a sound, l'il gal,' said the man, in a hoarse whisper. He sounded like an American! 'Don't you say I'm here. I'm just a poor man, lost and alone.'

Lucy-Ann couldn't believe her ears. She felt that she simply must call the others. But they didn't hear her, and as soon as she had shouted, the man frowned fiercely and shook his head.

'L'il gal, you gotta git away from here. It's a no-good mountain, full of bad men. They'll git you if you don't git away. There's bad things here, l'il gal.'

'What are you doing here?' asked Lucy-Ann, in a scared voice. 'How do you know all this?'

'I've been in that there bad mountain, l'il gal. I've gotten away. But this poor fellah's gotten no place to go – and he's surely scared by those big dogs. I'm staying right here in this nice big tree. You git away, l'il gal, git far away!'

Lucy-Ann felt odd, standing there talking to a black stranger up a tree. She suddenly turned and ran back to the others. She ran fast, and arrived absolutely out of breath.

'What's the matter, what's the matter?' cried Jack, seeing from Lucy-Ann's face that she had had a shock. Lucy-Ann could only gasp out one or two words. She pointed back to the stream.

'Black man!' she gasped. 'Black!'

'Black! That's what David said!' cried Philip. 'Get your breath, Lucy-Ann! Tell us what you saw. Quick!'

Lucy-Ann panted out what she had seen and heard. The others listened in astonishment. A black man hiding in a tree – from the dogs! A man who said the mountain was bad – an American – whatever did it mean?

'Come on – we'll ask him what he knows!' cried Jack. 'There's something going on here. We'd better find out and then we can tell Bill when he comes. Quick!'

They all ran back to the stream and peered up the tree. But there was nobody there. The man had gone.

'Blow!' said Jack, in disappointment. 'He must have seen you scuttle back to us, Lucy-Ann, to tell us you had seen him – and he's scared, and now he's gone.'

'It's a wonder the dogs didn't find him last night – and before that, when David saw him up this very same tree,' said Jack.

'Well, he's been rather clever, I think,' said Philip, looking at the stream. 'You know, dogs can't follow scent through water. They lose it. And I reckon that chap was clever enough to wade up or down the stream to that tree, and hop up it from the water. The dogs couldn't possibly follow his scent through the stream. They would lose it wherever he entered the water. Still, he must have felt pretty scared when he saw the dogs milling around near here!'

'Were they hunting for him, do you think?' asked Lucy-Ann fearfully. 'He must have been awfully afraid. I should be terrified if I thought a pack of Alsatian dogs was after me.'

The children hunted for the strange man, but he was nowhere to be seen. They wondered what he ate. There was not much to eat on the mountains except bilberries, wild raspberries and grass.

'Do you think he really meant there were men inside this mountain?' asked Dinah, when they had tired themselves out looking for the American.

'It seems incredible – but if you remember those noises of rumbling we heard yesterday – and the way the earth shook beneath us – it seems as if there *might* be men working underground,' said Jack.

'What – as miners or something?' asked Dinah.

'I don't know. Possibly. Though goodness knows what could be mined inside this mountain, or how they would get the machinery there. There would have to be a road – and then everyone would know.'

'It's very mysterious,' said Dinah.

Lucy-Ann sighed. 'It's another adventure, that's what it is. It's fatal to go off together like this. We go to look for birds, or butterflies or something – and we always stumble into something peculiar. I'm getting tired of it.'

'Poor Lucy-Ann!' said Philip. 'We certainly do happen on strange things. *I* think it's very exciting. I love adventures.'

'Yes, but I don't,' said Lucy-Ann. 'I don't like that kind of thing at all.'

'*I* do,' said Dinah at once. 'I've enjoyed every single one of our adventures. And this one seems more mysterious than any other. What *is* going on inside this mountain? How I'd love to know! If only we could see that chap again, we could ask him to tell us all about it.'

'Oh, listen – I do believe that rumbling's going to start again,' said Lucy-Ann suddenly. 'See how frightened Snowy is! Yes – there it comes.'

They sat and listened. Jack put his ear to the ground. At once the rumblings became magnified, and sounded more puzzling than ever. Was something exploding down there, far in the heart of the mountain?

Then the earth quivered as it had done before and Lucy-Ann clutched at Jack. It was horrible to feel the firm solid earth quivering like a jelly.

It soon stopped. Dinah glanced up at the steep mountain, rearing up just behind them, wondering what its secret was. She suddenly stiffened, and caught hold of Philip's arm.

'Look!' she said, and pointed upwards.

They all looked. Out of the side of the mountain was drifting a small cloud of smoke. One puff came. Then another. But it was not ordinary smoke. It was a curious crimson colour, and it did not drift away like mist on the wind, but hung like a solid little cloud, close to the mountain, for some time. Then it suddenly became lighter in colour and disappeared.

'Well – whatever was *that*?' said Jack, in amazement. 'I never in my life saw smoke like that before. There must be a vent or something in the side of the mountain there, that lets out smoke or gases.'

'What's a vent?' asked Lucy-Ann, her eyes looking as if they would drop out of her head.

'Oh – a sort of chimney,' said Jack. 'Somewhere with a draught that will take up smoke or gases to the outer air. Whatever's going on in the mountain produces that smoke, which has to be got rid of. I wonder what else is being produced inside there!'

Nobody could imagine. They couldn't seem to fit together all the curious facts they knew – the pack of man-hunting dogs – the poor runaway – the noises, the earth's shaking, the crimson smoke. It didn't make any sense at all.

'If only Bill would come!' said Philip. 'He might be able to fit this jigsaw together.'

'Or if we could get hold of that chap Lucy-Ann saw,' said Philip. 'He could tell us a lot.'

'We may see him again,' said Dinah. 'We'll watch out for him.'

They did see him again, that very evening – but alas, he didn't answer any of their questions!

14

Plenty of things happen

They decided to go for a walk that evening. They would leave Dapple tied up to a tree by the stream, with a note on his harness to say they would soon be back – just in *case* Bill came when they were away.

'Though he couldn't *possibly* be here yet,' said Jack. Still, you never knew with Bill. He had a remarkable way of doing impossible things extraordinarily quickly.

They went off together, Snowy capering about, and Kiki on Jack's shoulder. They climbed up past the cave where they had slept the night before. Their sleeping-bags were still there, pulled into the cave out of the sun. They meant to sleep in them up on the rock again that night.

'Let's follow Snowy,' suggested Dinah. 'He always seems to know a way to go, thought I expect he only follows his silly little nose! But he usually chooses quite possible paths for us.'

So they followed Snowy. The little kid took it into his

head to climb up the mountain, but at last they all came to such a steep cliff of rock, almost sheer, that they had to stop. Even Snowy was brought to a halt!

'I'm frightfully hot,' said Dinah, fanning herself. 'Let's sit down under those trees.'

The trees were waving about in the wind. Jack looked longingly up into the wind-blown branches. 'It would be lovely and cool up there, in the windy boughs,' he said. 'What about climbing up? They look pretty easy to climb.'

'A wizard idea!' said Philip. 'I love swinging in the branches at the top of a tree. Want a leg-up, Lucy-Ann?'

Lucy-Ann got a leg-up and soon they were all settled into forking branches, letting themselves be swung about in the wind, which was very strong just there.

'This is lovely,' said Dinah. 'Heavenly!'

'Super!' said Jack. 'Don't clutch my shoulder so tightly, Kiki. You won't fall off!'

Snowy was left down below, bleating. He tried his best to leap up into the tree but he couldn't. He ran round and round Philip's tree and then, in a rage, he tore up to a rock and leapt up it and down it without stopping. The children watched him, laughing at his antics.

Then, quite suddenly, a hullabaloo broke on their ears. It was the sound of excited barking and snarling, howling and yelping.

'The dogs!' said Jack, straining his eyes to see where the noise came from. 'I say – they're after that man!'

There came the crashing of bushes and twigs far below them on the mountain-side, accompanied by more howls and barks. Then the children caught sight of a man running across a bare stony part of the mountain-side below them – about half a mile away.

The dogs poured after him. Lucy-Ann almost fell out of her tree in fright at seeing a man chased by dogs. The children watched without a word, their hearts beating fast, anxious for the man to escape.

He came to a tree and flung himself up it just as the first dog reached him. He pulled himself up, and was lost to sight. The dogs surrounded the tree, clamouring loudly.

Lucy-Ann gulped. Tears ran down her face. She felt so sorry for the hunted man that she could hardly see through her tears. The others watched grimly. Philip debated whether to go down and see if he could call the dogs off.

Then another man appeared, walking leisurely across the mountain-side towards the tree and the dogs. He was too far away for the children to see what he was like, or to hear his voice.

But on the crisp air of the mountain came the shrill sound of a whistle. The dogs at once left the tree, and trotted back to the man. He stood not far off the tree, and evidently gave orders for the man to come down. But nobody came down from the tree.

The man waved his hand to the dogs and at once they

streamed back to the tree again, clamouring and howling like mad. The man turned to go back the way he came.

'Oh! He's left the dogs to keep the poor man up the tree till he starves, or comes down to be set on!' sobbed Lucy-Ann. 'Philip, what shall we do?'

'I'll go down and call the dogs off,' said Philip. 'I'll give the man a chance to get right out of sight, so that he won't see me. Then I'll see if I can get the dogs away and give that chap a chance to escape from the tree.'

He climbed down his tree, after he had waited for twenty minutes, to give the second man a chance to go back to wherever he had come from. He made his way cautiously through the tall bushes.

And then something happened. A rough hand pounced down on his shoulder and he was held in a grip like iron. He was swung round – and came face to face with the man who had ordered the runaway to come down from the tree!

Philip wriggled, but he couldn't possibly get away. He didn't dare to yell for the others in case they got caught too. Blow! Why hadn't he waited longer before going off to the black man's rescue!

'What are you doing here?' said the man, in a strange, foreign accent. 'Who are you, boy?'

'I've only come to look for butterflies,' stammered Philip, trying to look as if he knew nothing about any-thing but butterflies. He didn't like the look of the man at all. He had a fierce hawk-like face, overhanging eyebrows, and such a sharp look in his black eyes that Philip felt sure he would be difficult to deceive.

'Who are you with?' asked the man, digging his steel-like fingers into Philip and making him squirm.

'I'm alone, as you can see,' said Philip, hoping the man would believe him. The man looked at him searchingly.

'My dogs would have got you if you had been here for long,' he said. 'And all your friends too!'

'What friends?' asked Philip innocently. 'Oh, you mean Snowy, my kid? He always comes with me.'

Snowy had bounded up at that moment, to the obvious surprise of the man. 'He's like a dog – never leaves me. Let me go, sir. I'm looking for butterflies. I'll be gone tonight.'

'Where did you come from?' asked the man. 'Do your parents know where you are?'

'No,' said Philip truthfully. 'I just went away to hunt for butterflies. I came from over there.'

He nodded his head vaguely behind him, hoping that the man would think he was a harmless nature-lover, and let him go. But the man didn't.

Instead he tightened his fingers on Philip's shoulders, and turned towards the tree where the black man was still hiding, surrounded by the dogs.

'You'll come with me now,' he said. 'You've seen too much.'

Just then there came a yelling and shouting from the

tree. Evidently the runaway had given in. The man, still clutching Philip by the shoulder, and followed by a puzzled Snowy, went towards the tree. He took a whistle from his pocket and blew on it shrilly. As before, the dogs at once left the tree and came to him. The man shouted for the runaway to come down.

The poor man came down in such a hurry that he half fell. The dogs made no attempt to go for him. Philip saw that they had been extremely well trained.

The man fell on his knees and began to jabber something. He was terrified. The man told him to get up, in cold contemptuous tones. Surrounded by the dogs, the prisoner walked stumblingly in front of the man, who still held Philip firmly by the shoulder.

Up in their trees the children watched in horror, hardly believing their eyes when they saw Philip held by the man. 'Sh! Don't make a sound,' commanded Jack. 'It's no good us being captured too. If the dogs go with Philip, he'll be all right. He'll have ten friends he can call on at any time!'

The little procession of men, boy, dogs and kid passed almost beneath the trees the children were in. Philip did not glance up, though he longed to. He was not going to give away the hiding-place of the others.

Jack parted the branches of his tree and followed the procession anxiously with his eyes. They were going in the direction of the steep wall of unclimbable rock. Jack took up his field-glasses, which were slung round his neck as usual, and glued them to his eyes, following the company closely. Where exactly were they going? If he knew, he might be able to go and rescue Philip and Snowy.

He saw Philip taken right up to the steep wall. Then, before his eyes, the whole company seemed to vanish! One moment they were there – the next they were gone! Jack took his glasses from his eyes and rubbed the lenses, thinking something must have gone wrong with them. But no – he saw exactly the same thing – a steep wall of sheer rock – and nobody there at all, not even a dog!

'Jack! Can you see what's happened to Philip?' came Lucy-Ann's anxious voice. 'Oh, Jack – he's caught!'

'Yes, and he's been taken into that mountain,' said Jack. 'Though how, I don't know. One moment they were all there, the next they were gone! I can't understand it.'

He looked through his glasses again but there was nothing to be seen. He suddenly realized that the sun had gone down and it was getting dark. 'Girls! It'll be dark soon. We must get down and go to the cave, whilst we can still see our way!' said Jack. They all climbed down quickly. Lucy-Ann was trying to blink back tears.

'I want Philip to come back,' she said. 'What's happened to him?'

'Don't cry,' said Dinah. 'Crying won't help him! You always burst into tears when anything happens!'

Dinah spoke crossly because she was very near tears

herself. Jack put his arm round both of them. 'Don't let's quarrel. That won't help Philip. Come on, let's get back quickly. I'll fetch Dapple from the stream, and bring her up to the rock.'

They made their way back to the cave they had left their sleeping-bags in. Jack fetched the patient Dapple. Kiki sat silently on his shoulder. She always knew when things had gone wrong with the children. She nipped Jack's ear gently to tell him she was sorry.

It was almost dark when they reached the cave. There was no need to make a fire tonight – they did not fear wolves any more. Indeed they would have been very glad indeed to see dark figures come slinking up to the cave. They would have welcomed the dogs eagerly.

'I miss Snowy,' said Dinah. 'It's queer without him leaping about everywhere. I'm glad he's gone with Philip. I'm glad the slow-worm's gone too!'

They didn't want to get into the sleeping-bags and go to sleep. They wanted to talk. A lot of things seemed to be happening very suddenly. Oh dear – when would Bill come? They could manage quite well without grown-ups in many ways – but just at the moment all three would have welcomed even David!

'Well – let's get into our bags,' said Jack. 'Isn't the moon lovely tonight?'

'Nothing seems very nice when I think of Philip being captured,' said Lucy-Ann dismally. All the same, the moon was glorious, swinging up over the mountains, and making everywhere as light as day.

They were just about to slide into their bags when Lucy-Ann's sharp ears caught an unfamiliar sound.

'Listen!' she said. 'What's that? No, not a noise underground this time – somewhere up in the sky!'

They went out and stood on the flat rock, listening, their faces upturned to the moonlit sky.

'What a peculiar noise!' said Jack. 'A bit like an aeroplane – but *not* an aeroplane. What *can* it be?'

15

Behind the green curtain

The noise came nearer. 'Like a motor-bike in the sky,' said Jack.

'Or a sewing-machine,' said Dinah. 'Jack, look! What's that? That tiny speck up there?'

Jack fumbled for his glasses, which were still round his neck. He put them to his eyes, straining to focus the little black speck up in the moonlight. It came nearer.

'Well – whatever it is I do believe it's going to land on this mountain!' said Dinah. 'Isn't it going slowly? *Is* it an aeroplane, Jack?'

'No,' said Jack. 'Gosh – it's a helicopter! You know – they are just the thing for travelling in mountains. They don't fly fast but they can land in a very small space – on a lawn, or a roof even!'

'A *heli*copter!' cried Dinah, and took the glasses from Jack. 'Let me see.'

It was now near enough for Dinah to be able to see it clearly with the glasses. Jack and Lucy-Ann watched it with screwed-up eyes. It hovered over the mountain-top, and then flew slowly round it, appearing in sight again after a few minutes.

It then flew up a little higher, and descended slowly, almost vertically, its engine making a curious sound in the night. Then there was silence.

'It's landed,' said Jack. 'But where? Gosh, I wouldn't like to land on a mountain as steep as this one.'

'Perhaps there is a proper landing-place,' said Lucy-Ann. 'Right on the very top!'

'Yes. There may be,' said Jack. 'What a thing to do, though — land a helicopter on the very summit of a mountain like this! What for?'

Nobody knew the answer to that.

'Well,' said Jack, at last, 'if that helicopter *did* land up on top, that would be one way of bringing food and stuff to the men who are at work inside the mountain — they'd have to have food, and there's no way of getting it round about here!'

'I feel as if all this must be a dream,' said Lucy-Ann, in a small voice. 'I don't like it at all. I wish I could wake up.'

'Come on — let's get into our bags,' said Jack. 'We can't *do* anything. We'll just have to wait for Bill. We can sleep out on the rock tonight, if you like. It's got very warm again, and we're snug enough in our bags.'

Nibbling bars of chocolate the three of them slipped into the bags. Kiki flew up into a near-by bush. She cleared her throat as David had often done. 'Look you, whateffer, look you, whateffer,' she began, meaning to have a little practice of the new words she had learnt.

'Kiki! Shut up!' said Jack.

'Whateffer!' said Kiki, and hiccuped very loudly. 'Pardon!' she gave a cackle of laughter and said no more for a moment. Then she took her head out from under her wing. 'Pifflebunk,' she said, delighted at having remembered it, and put her head back again.

Jack woke several times in the night, wondering about Philip. He also puzzled his head to think how the whole company of dogs, men and boy could possibly have vanished as they did, under his very eyes. He felt that he really would have to go and explore that steep wall of rock the next day. Perhaps he would find out where the company had gone – and *how* it had gone.

'Do you think Bill will come today?' asked Lucy-Ann, next morning. Jack reckoned up and shook his head. 'No – perhaps he will tomorrow, though, if David got back quickly, and Bill came at once. Still – if we go far away from the stream, we'd better leave a note for Bill, in case he comes and we're not there. Like we did yesterday.'

They had taken the note off Dapple's harness the night before, when they had brought the donkey back from the stream, up to their sleeping-rock. Now Jack set to work to write another. In it he told the story of Philip's disappearance by the wall of rock, and he also wrote about the helicopter he had seen. He had a feeling that he had better tell all he knew in case – just in *case* – something happened, and he and the girls were captured too. So many strange things had happened on this mountain. It was quite likely that if the man got out of Philip the fact that he had friends near by the mountain, they would send to capture them too.

He took Dapple back to the stream, putting him in the shade, in some long lush grass, and near enough to the stream to stand in it, or drink if he liked. Dapple liked this kind of life well enough, but he stared anxiously all around, missing Snowy. Where was his tiny friend?

'Snowy will come back soon, Dapple,' said Jack, rubbing his hand up and down the long grey nose. 'You wait and see!'

'What are we going to do today?' asked Lucy-Ann, when Jack came back. 'I don't feel like doing anything now Philip's gone!'

'Well – would you like to come with me to the steep rocky wall the others went to last night?' said Jack. 'Just to see if we can find out how they disappeared so suddenly. But if you come we'll have to keep a jolly good look-out in case we're taken by surprise!'

Lucy-Ann looked as if she didn't want to come at all, but nothing would stop her being with Jack if she thought there was any likelihood of danger. If they were going to be taken by surprise, then she would be there too!

So, taking some tins with them in case they didn't feel inclined to go all the way back to the cave in the heat of the day for a meal, the three of them set off. Kiki flew over their heads, annoying the swallows, and crying 'Feetafeetit, feetafeetit!' just as they did. They took not the slightest notice of her, but went on with their fly-catching deftly and serenely.

The three came at last to the little copse of trees where they had swung in the wind the evening before. 'Wait here a minute,' said Jack, and he leapt up into a tree. 'I'll just have a look round to make sure the coast is clear.'

He balanced himself in branches near the top of the tree and swept the countryside around with his glasses. Not a sound was to be heard except the wind, the trees and the birds. There was no sign of any human being, or of any of the dogs.

'It seems all right,' said Jack when he got down to the foot of the tree again. 'We'll go. Come on.'

Kiki began to bray like Dapple, and Jack turned on her fiercely. 'Kiki! Stop it! Just when we want to be quiet! Bad bird! Silly bird!'

Kiki raised her crest up and down, snapped her beak angrily, and flew up into a tree. It was almost as if she had said, 'All right then – if you speak to me like that, I won't come with you!' She sat on a branch, sulking, keeping one eye on the three children walking towards the wall.

They reached it and looked upwards. It towered up,

steep and sheer. Nobody could climb that, not even Snowy!

'Now where were the others when they disappeared?' said Jack. 'About here, I think.'

He led the way to an uneven slab of rock. Hanging down in front of it, over the rocky wall, was a thick curtain of greenery, half bramble, half creepers of some kind, all matted together.

The children thought this mass of green was actually growing on the wall, in the same way that many other little plants and ferns grew. It was only when the wind blew strongly, and the curtain-like mass swung backwards and forwards a little that Lucy-Ann guessed it wasn't growing out of the wall – it was hanging down, covering it!

She caught hold of it. It swung back like a curtain! Behind it was the wall, right enough – but there was a split in it, a great crack that reached up about twenty feet.

'Look!' said Lucy-Ann. 'This is a kind of curtain, Jack. And look at the big crack in the wall behind. Is this where they went yesterday?'

'Gosh, yes! They must all have gone quickly behind this curtain of creepers,' said Jack. 'And I thought they had vanished! Hold it up, Lucy-Ann. Let's see the crack. I bet they went through that!'

All three passed easily behind the swinging curtain of creeper and bramble. They could slip through the crack without any trouble at all. Once through it they found themselves in an immensely high cave, very round, and with no roof that could be seen, though Jack flashed his torch up as far as he could manage.

'It's like a hole in the mountain,' he said. 'It goes up goodness knows how high!'

'Did the others come in here?' asked Dinah, staring upwards. 'Where did they go then?'

'Can't think,' said Jack, puzzled. 'I say, look here – look what's in the middle of the floor! I almost went into it!'

He flashed his torch on to the floor of the cave – but there was hardly any floor to be seen! Most of it was taken up by a silent black pool, whose surface had no wrinkle or ripple!

'It's not a nice pool,' said Lucy-Ann, with a shudder.

'This is a most peculiar cave,' said Dinah. 'No roof – no floor – only a deep pool! And no sign of where the others went yesterday.'

'There must be *some* way out,' said Jack, quite determined to search until he found it. He began to walk all round the cave, flashing his torch on it, inch by inch. But there was no opening anywhere, not even a tiny hole. The walls were absolutely solid.

'Well, there's no passage leading out of *this* cave!' said Jack, giving it up. He glanced up to the roofless top of the cave. 'The only way is up there! But there are no footholds to climb up – nothing! Nobody could possibly climb up these steep walls.'

'Well then – is there a way out through the pool?' said Dinah, half in fun.

Jack looked at the black pool. 'No, I don't see how that pool can possibly contain a way out of this cave. Still – it's the only thing I haven't examined. I'll have a swim in it – or wade across!'

But it was too deep to wade. Jack took two steps and the water came over his knees. He stripped off his clothes and plunged in. Lucy-Ann didn't like it much. She watched Jack anxiously as he swam across and back.

'Can't feel the bottom at all,' said Jack, kicking out with his legs. 'Must be awfully deep. A bottomless pool and a roofless cave – sounds odd, doesn't it? I'm coming out now. The water's icy cold.'

He found his footing almost at the edge of the pool, slipped and went in again. He reached out to grasp the edge and his hand found something else. It felt like a small steering-wheel under the water!

Jack got out and dressed. He was shivering too much to do any more investigation till he had some clothes on. Then he knelt down by the edge of the pool and put his hand in to feel the curious wheel-like thing again.

'Hold my torch, Lucy-Ann,' he commanded. 'There's something odd here!'

Lucy-Ann held the torch in trembling fingers. What was Jack going to find? 'It's a little wheel,' he said. 'Why is it here? Well, wheels are meant to turn, so I'll turn it! Here goes!'

He turned it to the right. It ran easily. And then he jumped violently because both the girls screamed loudly and clutched him hard!

16

Inside the mountain

'What's the matter?' shouted Jack, jumping up. 'What's happened!'

Lucy-Ann had dropped the torch in her fright. The light went out and they were in darkness. She clutched at Jack again and startled him.

'Something touched me!' she whispered. 'Something ran its fingers all down me. Oh, Jack, what was it?'

'Yes, and me too,' said Dinah, in a trembling voice. 'I felt them. They touched my shoulder softly and then ran all the way down to my feet. What is it, Jack? There's something here. Let's get out.'

'Where's the torch?' said Jack impatiently. 'Oh, Lucy-Ann, I hope it isn't broken. You idiot, dropping it like that.'

He groped about for it on the floor and found it. Luckily it hadn't rolled into the pool. He shook it and the light came on. Everyone was very thankful.

'Now, what touched you?' demanded Jack. 'Nothing touched *me*!'

'I don't know,' said Lucy-Ann. 'I want to get out of here, Jack. I'm frightened.'

Jack swung his torch round behind the girls. He saw something that made him cry out in surprise. The girls didn't dare to look. They clung to him, trembling.

'See what touched you? A rope-ladder falling down just behind you!' laughed Jack. 'Well, what a surprise! You'd never dream of that!'

Dinah pulled herself together at once, and forced herself to laugh. 'Well! Fancy that! I really did think it was somebody touching me. It felt just like it.'

'It must just have run down quietly behind you from somewhere up high,' said Jack, flashing his torch upwards, and following the ladder with the beam as far as he could. 'Well, you made *me* jump all right when you yelled. I almost went head-first into the pool!'

'It happened when you turned that wheel down there,' said Lucy-Ann, still shivering a little.

'Yes. A very clever little idea,' said Jack. 'I must say this is a jolly well-hidden entrance to the mountain – better even than Ali Baba's cave! First there's the green curtain. Then just a crack in the rock. Then you come in and see nothing but a black pool and a roofless cave. Most people would just say, "How odd!" and go out again!'

'Yes. They would never, never guess about the ladder

that comes tumbling down when you turn the wheel hidden so cleverly in the water,' agreed Dinah. 'Most ingenious, all of it. Somebody with brains lives in this mountain!'

'Yes,' said Jack thoughtfully. 'Brains that work and produce minor earthquakes and crimson smoke, and plan for landing-grounds for helicopters on mountain-tops – and keep packs of Alsatians that would terrorize anyone roaming too near the mountain. Very remarkable brains! I wonder exactly what those brains are after!'

The girls stared at him in the dimly lit cave, with the black pool glinting up at them. Jack sounded very serious. He felt serious too. There was something very strange about all this. Something very clever. Much too clever. What *could* be going on?

He stared up the ladder. He felt very much inclined to go up it. He longed to see what was inside the mountain – and he wanted to find Philip again too. Then a hollow voice made them all jump violently.

'Naughty boy! Pifflebunk!'

'It's Kiki,' said Jack, relieved. 'You wretched bird, you made me jump! What do you think of this cave, Kiki?'

'Pifflebunk,' repeated Kiki, and made a noise like a mowing-machine. It sounded terrible in that roofless cave. The noise seemed to go up and up endlessly. Kiki enjoyed the sound. She began all over again.

'Be quiet,' said Jack. 'Goodness knows what will

happen if your noises arrive at the top of this ladder, and somebody hears them!'

'You're not going up, are you, Jack?' asked Lucy-Ann, afraid, as she saw Jack place a foot on the lowest rung of the rope-ladder.

'Yes. I'll just go up to the top and see what's there and come down again,' said Jack. 'I don't expect there'll be anyone on guard, because nobody would ever dream of us guessing the secret of getting the ladder down. You two go out into the sunshine and wait for me.'

'No. We're coming too,' said Lucy-Ann. They had lost Philip. She wasn't going to lose Jack! So she and Dinah began to climb up behind him.

The ladder was well made and strong. It swung to and fro a little as the three of them climbed it. Up they went, and up and up. There seemed no end to it!

'I'm stopping for a rest,' whispered Jack. 'You stop too. It's frightfully tiring, this.'

They clung to the rungs and rested, panting a little with their long climb. Lucy-Ann didn't like to think how far away the foot of the cave was. Nor did she like to think how far away the top of the ladder was!

They went on again. It was pitch dark, for Jack had put away his torch, needing both hands to climb with. Lucy-Ann began to feel that she was in a peculiarly hor-rid nightmare – one in which she would have to climb ladders in the dark until she awoke in the morning!

'I say – I can see a dim sort of light now,' whispered

Jack. 'I believe we must be coming to the top. Don't make any noise.'

They got to the top just as Lucy-Ann felt that her arms would not hold on to the ladder any longer. As Jack said, there was a dim light there. He climbed off on to a rocky floor, and the girls followed. They all lay panting for a few minutes, unable even to look round and see where they were.

Jack recovered first. He sat up and gazed round him. He was in a little chamber, lighted by a dim lamp. Big stone jugs full of what looked like water stood at the back, with mugs near by. Jack's eyes gleamed. Just what they wanted after their terrible climb! He fetched a jug and three mugs and the three of them drank deeply of the ice-cold water.

'Now I feel better,' said Jack, with a sigh. He put back the jug and mugs. There was nothing else to see in the room at all. At the far end was an open passage-way, leading into the heart of the mountain.

Jack went to it. Lucy-Ann called softly to him. 'Jack! Aren't you coming back? You said you'd only go to the top and look!'

'Well, I'm looking,' said Jack. 'There's a narrow passage here. Come and see. I wonder where it leads to.'

The girls went to see. Jack wandered along a little way and the girls followed, not liking to be left alone. They came to another dim lamp, set on a rocky shelf in the passage wall. Jack went on and on, following the winding passage, coming to lamp after lamp that lighted the way.

'Come back now,' whispered Lucy-Ann, pulling at his sleeve. 'We've gone far enough.'

But Jack felt that he couldn't possibly go back now. Why, he might meet Philip round the next corner! So on he went.

They came to a forking of the passage, which suddenly divided into three. The children stopped, wondering where the three passages led to. They all looked exactly the same to them.

And then, out of one passage capered somebody they knew very well indeed. It was Snowy!

The kid was as delighted to see them as they were to see him. He butted them all, rubbed his nose into their hands, and bleated joyfully. Jack felt pleased.

'We'll follow Snowy,' he said to the girls. 'He'll lead us to Philip!'

So they let the little kid dance in front of them, leading the way. He led them down the passage, into a vast, hall-like cave, into another passage, and then, to their great surprise, they came to a most amazing place.

It was like a vast laboratory, a work-room set in the heart of the mountain. It lay below them, and they had to lean over a little gallery to look at it.

'What is it?' whispered Lucy-Ann, awed at the amount of curious things there. There was no enormous machinery – only a vast network of gleaming wires, great glass jars standing together, crystal boxes in which sparks and flames shot up and down, and rows upon rows of silently spinning wheels that shone strangely as they spun. The wires ran from these all over the place.

In the middle of the work-room shone a curious lamp. It had many sides, and it glowed first one colour and then another. Sometimes it was so dazzling that the children could hardly look at it. Sometimes it died down to a faint red, green or blue glow. It seemed alive – a monster eye that watched over everything in that secret laboratory.

The children gazed, fascinated. There was nobody there at all. Everything seemed to work on its own, never stopping. The wheels spun round, the wires gleamed, and nothing made any noise beyond a very quiet humming.

And then – and then there began that faint, far-off rumbling they knew so well. Far below the laboratory, deep deep down, came a stirring and a groaning, as something happened in the depths of the mountain. Then, as had happened before, the mountain quivered a little, and shook, as if something tremendous had happened deep underground.

The great lamp in the middle suddenly grew bright, so bright that the children crouched back, afraid. It grew crimson, the brightest crimson they had ever seen in their lives. It began to belch out tiny puffs of crimson smoke.

Jack began to choke. He pushed the girls back into the passage, and they breathed the fresher air there in relief. Snowy, frightened, crouched against them.

'That's the smoke we saw coming out of a hole in the side of the mountain,' whispered Jack. 'There must be a chimney-pipe built from that lamp, right away up the mountain to the hole, where the smoke can escape.'

'What's going on, do you think?' asked Dinah, in awe. 'What's all that wire for, and the crystal boxes and things?'

'I haven't the least idea,' said Jack. 'But it's plain that it's something very secret, or they'd never do all this here, in this lonely, inaccessible place.'

'Atom bombs or something, do you think?' asked Lucy-Ann, with a shiver.

'Oh, no – you want enormous buildings for that,' said Jack. 'No – it's something very odd and unusual, I should think. Let's go back and peep.'

They went back, but everything was just as it had been, the wheels spinning silently, the crystal boxes sparking and flaming up and down inside, the great lamp watching like an eye, now crimson, now blue, now green, now orange.

'Let's go round the gallery and see where it goes to,' whispered Jack. 'I feel as if I'm in some sort of Aladdin's cave now – the Slave of the Ring might appear at any moment!'

They wandered on and came to another extraordinary

place. It was really only a high-roofed cave – but it was made into a great, sumptuous hall, with flights of steps leading up to what looked like a throne. Beautiful hangings hung down the walls from the roof, which glittered with shining lamps shaped like stars.

The floor was laid with a golden carpet, and ranged on each side were beautiful chairs. The children stared in astonishment.

'Whatever's all this?' whispered Dinah. 'Does some king live here? The king of the mountain!'

17

Philip again

'It's peculiar there's nobody about at all,' said Jack, staring round at the silent hall. 'Not a soul to be seen! I wonder where everyone is. All those wheels and wires and things whirring away busily by themselves, with nobody to see to them – and now this great empty place, with its throne and gorgeous hangings!'

'Jack!' said Dinah, pulling at his sleeve. 'Can't we find Philip now and rescue him? We've only got to go back through those long passages and down the rope-ladder! Snowy will take us to Philip, and we can take him safely to the entrance of the mountain.'

'Yes. That's a good idea,' said Jack. He stroked the little white kid by his side. 'Where's Philip?' he whispered, and gave Snowy a push. 'You show us, Snowy.'

Snowy butted Jack gently. He didn't seem to know what the boy meant. Jack gave it up after a bit. 'We'll wait and see if Snowy goes off by himself,' he said. 'If he does, we'll follow him.'

So they waited. Snowy soon became restive and set off down the big hall past the great throne. The children followed cautiously, keeping by the walls, as far in the shadows as possible. Snowy disappeared through some deep red curtains. The children peeped through them. On the other side was what looked like a small library. Books lined the walls. The children looked at the titles curiously. They could not understand what any of them meant. Most of them were in foreign languages, and all of them looked very learned and difficult.

'Scientific books,' said Jack. 'Come on. Snowy has gone through that opening.'

They followed him. He saw that they were coming and waited for them. They hoped he was taking them to Philip!

He was! He led them upwards through a curiously rounded tunnel-like passage, lit at intervals by the same kind of dim lamps they had seen in the first passages. It was weird going along in the half-dark, not able to see very far in front or behind. Snowy trotted in front like a little white ghost.

They passed big openings filled with what looked like stores of some kind. Boxes, chests, packages of all kinds were there, flung in higgledy-piggledy.

Jack paused to examine some. There were foreign labels on most of them. One had been opened, showing tins of food.

'Look,' said Jack, 'it's what I said. They have their

food brought here – by the helicopter, I expect. I wonder what in the world they're up to.'

They came to some steps hewn out of the rock itself. These led upwards rather steeply in a spiral. Snowy bounded up lightly, but the others panted as they went up and up, twisting and turning with the spiral of the stairway.

They came to a door set fast in the side of the stone stairway. It was a stout wooden door, with great bolts on the outside. Snowy stopped beside this door and bleated loudly.

Then the children's hearts jumped as they heard a familiar voice. 'Snowy! I'm still here! I can't get to you, Snowy, but never mind!'

'That's Philip!' said Jack. He knocked gently on the door. 'Philip! It's us! We're going to undo the bolts of this door.'

There was an astonished exclamation, and the sound of feet running across to the door. Then Philip's excited voice came through the door, eager and thrilled.

'Gosh, Jack! Is it really you? Can you let me out?'

Jack shot the bolts back. They were well oiled and went back easily. Philip pulled him into the space beyond as soon as the door was open. The girls followed too, with Snowy.

'Jack! How did you get here? I've been shut in this strange place with that black man. Look, there he is, over there. He sleeps most of the time. He's the one the dogs were after.'

Sure enough, there was the man, lying against the side of the cave, fast asleep. Jack and the girls looked round Philip's prison in wonder.

It was nothing but a cave in the side of the top of the mountain. It opened on to the sky . . . or so it seemed! At first the children could see nothing but a vast expanse of blue when they gazed out of the opening opposite to the door.

'It's almost at the top, this cave,' said Jack. 'Isn't it a miraculous view? You can see right over the tops of the mountains yonder. I've never been so high in my life before. It makes me quite giddy to look out for long.'

Dinah stepped to the edge of the cave but Philip pulled her back. 'No, don't go too near. There's an almost sheer drop there. And if you look down it makes you feel very strange – as if you're on top of the world and might fall any minute!'

'Hold my hand then, whilst I look,' said Dinah, and Jack wanted to see too.

'Lie down on the floor of the cave and look out of it that way,' said Philip. 'You feel safer then.'

So all four lay down and peered over the edge of the cave that was almost at the top of the mountain. It certainly gave them a curious feeling. Far far down below were the slopes of the mountain, and far below that the valley. Lucy-Ann clutched Philip tightly. She felt as if she was toppling over downwards! But she wasn't, of course. She was safe on the floor of the cave. It was just the terrific feeling of height that made her think she must be falling down and down!

'I don't like it,' she said, and came away from the ledge. The others were awed. They gazed until they too felt that they were going to fall, and then they pushed themselves back and sat up.

'Come with us quickly,' said Jack to Philip. 'We know the way out – and Snowy will guide us if we don't! We must go whilst there's a good chance. The whole place seems deserted. It's most peculiar.'

'Well, the men live on the very top of the mountain,' said Philip. 'The American has been telling me quite a lot. This cave is very near the top – so near that I can sometimes hear men talking and laughing. There must be a plateau on the summit – or some kind of flat place – because the helicopters land there.'

'Oh! Well, I suppose everyone must be up on the mountain-top then!' said Jack. 'We didn't meet a soul coming up here. Come on, let's go, Philip. Don't let's waste a minute. We can tell each other everything when we're safely out of this extraordinary mountain.'

They all went to the door – and then Jack pushed the others back quickly. He shut the door quietly and put his finger to his lips.

'I can hear voices!'

So could the others. Loud voices that were coming

nearer their door. Would the owners of the voices spot that the bolts were undone?

The voices came nearer and nearer – and then passed! Evidently nobody had looked at the bolts of the door. The children breathed again.

'Thank goodness! They've gone past!' said Jack. 'Shall we wait for a few minutes and then run for it?'

'No. Wait till the men come back and go up to the roof,' said Philip. 'I think they are only the paratroopers gone to get some stores to take up to the top.'

Everyone stared at him. '*Para*-troopers!' said Jack, in amazement. 'What do you mean? Why should there be paratroopers here?'

'This chap told me. His name's Sam,' said Philip, nodding towards the sleeping man. 'Let's wait till those fellows come back with their stores, or whatever they've gone to fetch. I don't think they'll even look at this door. They don't know I'm here!'

'Well – for goodness' sake tell us all about everything then,' said Jack, filled with intense curiosity. 'Paratroopers! It sounds impossible.'

'Well, you know when I was caught, don't you?' began Philip. 'They took me to that steep wall, behind a thick screen of creeper, and in at an opening there. I was pushed up some kind of ladder in the dark – a rope-ladder, I should think – and we went up for ages and ages.'

The others nodded. They knew all about that.

'We went through long passages, and came to a jolly frightening place – with wheels and things . . . Did you see it too?'

'Yes. Most extraordinary. But there was no one there,' said Jack.

'I didn't have time to see much,' said Philip. 'Then we went round a gallery – the one that looks down on that place of wheels and wires and sparks and flames – and came into a most magnificent place – like a room out of a palace!'

'Yes – we saw it too. A room for a king, with a throne and all,' said Jack. 'But nobody there!'

'Well, then I was pushed up passages and steps to this cave,' said Philip. 'And I was bolted in, and here I've stayed ever since! This man was pushed in too – but poor little Snowy was bolted out! He's come and bleated out-side my door dozens of times. I hated that. He sounded so lost and miserable.'

Snowy was very happy now, however! He was curled up on Philip's knee, occasionally butting him gently to get a little more attention.

'I've had food pushed in through the door – all tinned stuff,' said Philip. 'But nobody's said a word to me, not even that nasty foreign-looking fellow who caught me. You should see his eyes! You often read in books about people with piercing eyes. Well, he's *really* got them – they go right through you! I was glad he didn't question me much, because I felt as if he'd know everything by reading my very thoughts.'

The others had been listening intently. Jack nodded towards the sleeping man. 'What did he tell you?'

'Oh, a lot of peculiar things,' said Philip. 'He said he saw an advertisement in the paper asking for men who had been paratroopers – you know, men who are trained to jump out of planes high in the air, and parachute to earth.'

'Yes. Go on,' said Jack, impatiently.

'Well, the hawk-eyed man – the one who captured me – he goes by the name of Meier, by the way – interviewed him at some office in Mexico, and offered him a terrific sum of money if he'd come and try some new kind of parachute-jumping.'

'What kind?' asked Dinah.

'I don't exactly know. Sam sounded a bit muddled when he told me – or else I didn't understand him,' said Philip. 'It's something to do with flying through the air on *wings* – wings fixed to his arms. Apparently you can't possibly fall to earth when you've got these wings on, and you can guide yourself where and how you like – just as birds do.'

'That's impossible,' said Jack at once. 'Quite mad.'

'Yes. That's why I think Sam got hold of the wrong idea,' said Philip. 'Well – this fellow Meier engaged a whole lot of ex-paratroopers, paid them fabulous sums, and brought them here, in helicopters, to the top of this mountain. And their job is to try out these wings – or so Sam says.'

'Has he tried them?' asked Jack.

'No. But three of his mates have. They had these peculiar wings fitted to their arms and were given orders to jump from the helicopter at a given moment – or else be pushed out,' said Philip.

'What happened?' asked Jack.

'Sam doesn't know,' answered Philip. 'You see, none of his mates came back. He's pretty certain they fell to their deaths. *He* didn't want to do the same – so he got away.'

18

A little exploring

There was a long pause after this strange story. It was very hard to believe – and yet they had seen and heard such strange things the last few days that they felt anything might be true of this lonely mountain.

'But what's the idea?' asked Jack, after a while. 'And why all the wheels and wires and things? I just don't get the hang of it all.'

'Nor do I. But Sam reckons that if the experiment came off, and men could really fly with these wings, somebody would make a most colossal fortune!' said Philip. 'Everyone would want them. Everyone would fly.'

'It sounds lovely,' said Lucy-Ann. 'I should love to fly like the birds do – much, much better than going in an aeroplane!'

They all felt the same – but nobody could really believe in these 'wings' that Sam had talked of.

'How did he escape?' asked Jack, nodding at the black man.

'He did an absolutely mad thing – as dangerous as jumping off a helicopter to try the "wings",' said Philip. 'He got a parachute out of the stores, came in here, fitted it on – and jumped!'

Everyone shuddered. 'What! Jumped out of this cave, right from the top of the mountain?' said Jack. 'Gosh, he's a brave man!'

'He is. His parachute opened, and he floated down to earth, landing with an awful bump. But of course he'd learnt how to fall, and he soon recovered. The next thing was – to find safety somewhere.'

'He couldn't have found a lonelier, more deserted bit of country than in these mountains,' said Jack. 'I suppose he didn't even know where he was.'

'He hadn't the faintest idea,' said Philip. 'I told him we were in Wales – but he didn't know where that was.'

'And then the dogs got after him, I suppose?' said Jack. 'Poor Sam!'

'Yes. He knew about them, because they live up on the mountain-top with the men. He says they're used to scare any possible wanderer who comes near this mountain – and, of course, to hunt anyone who does escape – or find anyone who crashes if the wings don't work.'

'That's more likely,' said Jack. 'Gosh, what a horrible, callous lot of men there must be behind all this! I never heard of anything like it in my life.'

'Sam says there's a king,' said Philip. 'The king of the mountain! Isn't it incredible? That throne must be for him. Sam's never seen him. He must be the spider at work, catching all these fellows and making them try out his mad experiments.'

'We thought there was some colossal brain behind all this,' said Jack. 'I suppose that hawk-eyed man – Meier – isn't the king, is he?'

'Oh, no! I don't know what you'd call him – sort of organizer, I suppose. He sees to everything – the stores – all the arrangements – shuts up the men when the helicopters arrive – and so on. There are two men, apparently, who work together on these things. The king is somebody who only appears on state occasions – such as when another pair of wings is produced, and the men have to go down to that great stateroom, listen to some speech they don't understand, and watch one of their number being picked to try out the wings.'

'Picking out a victim for sacrifice, it sounds like!' said Jack grimly. 'I don't like this at all. It's so *mad*.'

'Sam was ill the last time the king picked out his victims,' said Philip. 'So he hasn't seen the king of the mountain, as I said. He must be a twisted sort of chap – really callous and cruel, to make these fellows try out wings that can't possibly be any good.'

'I agree with you!' said Jack. 'And I think the sooner we get out of here and get into touch with old Bill, the better. I don't feel safe in this mountain. No wonder

Lucy-Ann got "feelings" about it. I've got quite a lot of feelings about it myself now!'

'Look – Sam's waking up,' said Lucy-Ann. They all looked at the man. He sat up, and rubbed his eyes. He looked across the cave and seemed surprised to see so many children.

Then he recognized Lucy-Ann as the little girl who had seen him up in the tree. He smiled, and then shook his head.

'Didn't I tell you to git away,' said Sam, looking solemn. 'This here is a bad mountain. Those men are bad, too.'

'We're going now, Sam,' said Philip. 'As soon as we think it's safe. Will you come too? We know the way out.'

Sam looked frightened. 'I'm scared of those dogs,' he said. 'I reckon I'm safe right here.'

'You're not. I bet you'll be the very next one chosen to try out the "wings" you told me about,' said Philip.

'The wings're better than those dogs,' said Sam.

Voices came past the door. The children fell silent and listened till they had gone past. Sam listened too.

'That was Pete and Jo,' he said.

'Well, Pete and Jo have gone up to the mountain-top again,' said Jack. 'Come on. It seems a good time to go now. We didn't meet anyone coming here – and the chances are we shan't meet anyone going back. What a tale we'll have to tell Bill!'

They opened the door cautiously. Snowy bounded out at once. Kiki was on Jack's shoulder, having kept silent for a surprisingly long time. She did not seem to like this peculiar mountain!

They went quietly down the spiral stairway, following its many turns round and round. They came to the openings where the stores were kept. It made them feel very hungry to see all the tins of food; but there was no time to think of eating now. They had to escape as quickly as possible.

Snowy led them down the dimly lit passages. The children expected to see the curious library of books at the end of them, but Snowy had apparently taken them a different way. They stopped after a while in dismay.

'I say – this isn't right. We didn't see that cave there before – I'm sure we didn't!' said Jack. They hesitated, not knowing whether to go on or go back. It would be awful to get lost in the heart of the mountain!

'I can hear some kind of noises,' said Lucy-Ann, listening. 'Let's creep on and see what they are.'

They went on down a wide passage that at times ran very steeply downhill. The air suddenly grew hot.

'Phew!' said Philip, mopping his forehead. 'I can hardly breathe.'

They came out on a kind of balcony that overlooked a great deep pit, so vast that it took the children's breath away. Far down in the middle of it men were at work, though what they were doing the children couldn't possibly tell. They were as small as ants.

Great lamps lit up the pit. The children gazed in astonishment. What *could* be going on down there?

Suddenly Jack nudged Philip. 'Look – the men have slid aside the floor of the pit – do you see? What's that under it?'

Jack might well ask! Out of the hole in the pit floor shone a brilliant mass of colour – but a colour the children did not know! It was not blue or green, not red or yellow, not any colour they had ever seen before. They gaped at it in surprise.

Then, suddenly they felt a curious feeling – a feeling of lightness, as if they were in a dream, and not quite real. They clutched the balcony rail, afraid. At the same moment the men down below slid the great floor over the hole in the pit again, and shut out the brilliant mass of unknown colour. At once the strange feeling passed away from the children, and they were themselves once more.

They felt a little weak. 'Let's go,' said Jack, scared. 'I don't like this.'

But before they could go there began that now familiar rumbling noise from the very depths of the mountain! The children clung to one another. It was so much louder now that they were *inside* the mountain. It was louder than thunder, an angry, unearthly noise. Then the balcony they were on began to shake.

Jack took one last look down into the strange pit. The men had disappeared – probably hidden safely behind rocky walls. Jack caught Lucy-Ann's hand and fled! After him came Philip and Dinah. Kiki clung to Jack's shoulder, more scared than any of them. Snowy had disappeared completely.

The four children tore up the steep wide passage that had led them down to the pit. The floor of it shook beneath their feet as they ran. The children felt sure that the whole of the great mountain was shaking. What powers were being used by these men? Surely they must have discovered some scientific secret unknown to anyone before!

The children did not stop running until they came to the end of the uphill passage. They were streaming with perspiration, and panting loudly. Snowy suddenly joined them and pressed against Philip's legs. All four children sank down in a heap and Snowy walked over them, unheeded.

'For goodness' *sake* let's get out of here,' said Philip at last. 'I daresay if we were scientists we shouldn't be a bit scared, only intensely interested – but all I can say is – let's get out of here!'

Everyone agreed heartily. The only thing was – which was the way? They got up and walked along a twisty little passage. It forked into two after a bit, and the children, not knowing which to take, took the right-hand one. It led them to a cell-like cave with a narrow bed in it, a jug and basin, and a shelf. Nothing more.

'Funny!' said Jack. 'I expect it belongs to Meier, or one of the other men. Let's go back.'

They went back to where the passage forked, and took the left-hand way. To their great surprise they came to hanging curtains of purple silk, patterned with great red dragons!

They stopped. Philip put his hand on Snowy to prevent him from darting forward. Jack crept to the curtains on tiptoe.

Beyond was a cave so beautifully decorated, so profusely hung with curtains and spread with thick carpets that it didn't seem like a cave at all. A couch stood in one corner, covered with a purple silk quilt, worked with the same red dragons as on the curtains they had seen.

Jack stared. Perhaps this was where the king slept. It felt deliciously cool here. Where did the little cooling draught come from? He saw a narrow rod hanging on the wall near him, with slits in it all the way along. He put his hand up and felt a draught of air. How astonishing! It was only a rod fixed to the wall. How could fresh air come out of it? Again Jack felt that there were remarkably ingenious brains at work in this mountain.

He heard voices from a room further on whose opening was hidden by the same kind of purple curtains that hung in other places. He tiptoed back to the others.

'We'll wait for a bit. There's somebody talking in the

room beyond this one. This is the king's bedroom, I should think.'

They waited, peeping through the curtains every now and then. They all began to feel terribly hungry. They were very relieved when the voices stopped and there was silence. They tiptoed through the bedroom and into the room beyond.

They stopped in delight – not at the strange beauty of the room – but at the gorgeous food on the table!

19

The king of the mountain

'Look at that!' said Jack. 'Somebody's been having a meal here – three people – and look at what they've left!'

'Can't we have some?' said Lucy-Ann, eyeing a great bowl of fresh strawberries and a jug half full of cream. Near by was a plate of cooked lobsters, and two dishes of mixed salads.

It was clear that three people had been having a meal there, judging by the plates and glasses, all of which were really beautiful.

'I call this a feast – a royal feast!' said Dinah, and she picked up a cake with cream icing on the top in the shape of a rose, and dug her teeth into it. 'I don't know who this stuff belongs to – but there's nobody to ask permission to share it – and I'm too hungry to wait!'

'So am I! We'll get Bill to pay for it if anyone objects,' said Jack, and set to work on a lobster. There were dishes of things the children had never seen before. They tasted one or two, but they were spiced in a way they disliked.

There were peaches and nectarines, pineapples and plums of all kinds. 'The helicopter must be pretty busy bringing all these!' said Philip, biting into the sweetest peach he had ever tasted in his life. 'I must say the King of this mountain does himself proud!'

Nobody came to interrupt them at all. Kiki feasted well, enjoying the food as much as the children. Snowy ate all the salad offered him, and for a treat was allowed to be on Philip's knee, with his forefeet on the table. He badly wanted to get on the table itself, and could not understand why Kiki was allowed there when he wasn't.

'If you eat any more, Kiki, you'll get the hiccups properly!' said Jack. 'Stuffing yourself like that! Greedy!'

'Pop goes Polly,' agreed Kiki, and would have given a cackle of laughter if Jack hadn't shushed her.

'Well – what about trying to find our way out again?' said Jack at last. 'I don't know whether it's anything to do with that strange feeling we had when the floor of the big pit was pushed back, and we saw that extraordinary mass of brilliance below – but I feel rather don't-carish now – not scared any more. I don't even feel that it's terribly urgent to get out of here, though I know it is!'

'It was a very unusual feeling,' said Philip. 'I thought I was going to float up into the air the next minute! I hung on to that balcony for dear life!'

They had all felt the same – and now they felt as Jack did – very 'don't-carish'. But that wouldn't do at all – it was imperative that they should find their way out as soon as possible.

They left the curious dining-room, with its laden table. They went into a passage that was much more brightly lit than the others they had walked down. Hangings decorated the rocky walls, great curtains that swayed a little in the draught that ran through the passages.

'This must be the king's own quarters,' said Jack. 'Maybe we shall come to the throne-room soon.'

He was quite right. They did. But this time the throne-room was not empty. It was full!

Men stood there silently. There were all kinds, and a tough-looking lot they were! They were of many nationalities. Some had the maroon beret that paratroopers have when in uniform. The peeping children thought that probably they were all old paratroopers. There were about twenty of them. Sam was there too, and Philip gave a little start when he saw him. Now it would be known that he, Philip, had escaped! Whoever had gone to bring Sam down here would have seen the unbolted door and found that he was gone.

Blow! Now he would be carefully hunted for, and it would be very difficult to escape. He nudged Jack and pointed out Sam to him. Jack, peeping through the curtains that hung before them, nodded and frowned. The same thought occurred to him as had occurred to Philip.

He debated whether to go off straight away now and

try to find the way out. But either they would have to go back the way they had just come, which obviously would not take them to the entrance they knew – or else they would have to go into the throne-room – where they would certainly be seen. No – they would have to stop where they were till this meeting, or whatever it was, was over.

Besides the paratroopers there were guards, men who looked like soldiers standing in an elaborate uniform down each side of the great hall. The throne was empty. There was no sign of the man Meier.

But suddenly there came a whispering among the men gathered there. The great curtains near the throne were flung back by two soldiers and the king of the mountain entered!

He seemed very tall, for he had a great crown that stood up from his head, embroidered with glittering stones. His wore a rich suit and cloak, and looked more like an Indian prince at some splendid festival than anything else. His yellowish face looked out impassively from below his great crown, and a mass of black hair swung down on each side. He sat down on the throne.

Beside him stood two men. Philip was sure that one was Meier. He didn't know the other, but he didn't like the ape-like face and enormous, burly figure. Meier's hawk-like eyes swept the room. He began to speak in a penetrating, most incisive voice, in a language that the children did not know. Then he paused and spoke in English.

The children listened, spell-bound. Meier spoke of the king and the wonderful gift he was giving to mankind – the gift of flying. He spoke of the grand men who were helping them in their experiment – the para-troopers willing to try the 'wings'. He spoke of the great wealth the men would receive, the honours that would be piled on them. Then he said it all again in a third language and then in a fourth.

He seemed to hypnotize everyone as he spoke. Jack could not help feeling that a lot he said was sheer non-sense – but he couldn't do anything but believe it whilst he heard it, and it was obvious that all the men there drank every word in, whether it was spoken in their own language or not. What a spell-binder, thought Jack!

Then volunteers were called for. All the men stepped forward at once. The king then rose and, apparently at random, picked out two or three. He spoke a few inaud-ible words in an unexpectedly thin, reedy voice that didn't seem to go at all with his kingly presence.

Then Meier took charge again. He said that these men, among the first to fly with wings, would be sent back to their own countries after the experiment, with wealth enough to last them for a lifetime. All the others who had tried out the wings were now safely back in their homes, and were rich and honoured men.

'I *don't* think!' muttered Jack to Philip, remembering what Sam had related.

The king then walked majestically out and Meier and the other man followed. The guards ushered the paratroopers away and soon the great throne-room was empty.

When everyone had gone and there was complete silence, Jack whispered to Philip, 'We know the way out from here. Come on!'

They went to the huge laboratory, where the wheels and wires were still at their secret work. The children stood in the gallery above the big work-room and looked down at the strange lamp in the middle. Dinah suddenly clutched Jack and made him jump. He looked at her.

She pointed to where there was a great cluster of glass jars, with tubes running from one to the other. Jack saw somebody there.

It was an old man with a very large forehead, larger and rounder than any forehead Jack had seen in his life. The man was quite bald, which made his head seem more curious than ever. He bent over the glass jars and looked searchingly into them.

'Come on before he sees us,' whispered Jack, and pulled the others towards the passages that would lead them to the entrance. They went along them and at last came to the little chamber where the pitchers of water and the mugs were. Now to get down the rope-ladder and escape!

'What about Snowy?' whispered Dinah. 'How can we get him down?'

'I wonder how he got up before?' said Philip. 'And the dogs too. I never thought of that. I was just pushed up in the dark, and I was so scared I didn't think of Snowy or the dogs. They couldn't have climbed that ladder!'

'There's probably some hole somewhere that they went into,' said Dinah. 'A hole outside, I mean – too small for us, but big enough for Snowy and the dogs.'

As it turned out afterwards, Dinah was right. There *was* a small hole near the crack, and it was through this and up a narrow little tunnel that Snowy had passed with the dogs, who knew the way very well. The dogs' tunnel led eventually into one of the passages, and that was how Snowy had got into the mountain but had not been imprisoned with Philip.

Snowy was still with them. He knew the way he had come in by, but he wasn't going to leave the others. Jack switched on his torch and felt above for the rope-ladder.

'Where is the wretched thing?' he said. 'Surely it was just here!'

Snowy came and pressed close to him, and nearly sent him headlong down to the black pool. 'Hold Snowy!' he said to Philip. 'I almost went over then. I can't seem to find the ladder. It should be hanging down somewhere about here.'

'Let *me* look,' said Philip, giving Snowy to Dinah. He felt about too, and Jack flashed his torch all round and

169

about to see if he could spy the rope-ladder up which they had all come.

But it wasn't there – or if it was, nobody could see it! Jack flashed his torch down into the hole as far as he could. No ladder at all!

'What's happened to it?' he said, exasperated.

'Perhaps someone has turned that little wheel in the pond the *other* way – and the ladder rolled up and put itself away,' suggested Dinah.

This was a dreadful thought. Jack began to look round the little chamber to see if the rope-ladder had been pulled up by the machinery set in motion by the wheel – but he couldn't see it anywhere.

His hand touched a spike on the wall. He focused his torch on it. 'This may be a lever!' he said to the others. 'Look!'

He pulled and pressed at the spike, and it suddenly gave way, pulling downwards. A slab of rock was moved smoothly – and there behind was the rope-ladder! How it worked with the wheel below the children could not imagine.

It certainly wouldn't work with them. It was evidently coiled or folded neatly in the hollow behind the rock – but how to get it from there nobody could make out. It needed some machinery put in motion to set it free. Then, Jack supposed, it would come sliding smoothly out of the place it was in, fall over the edge of the rock, and uncoil all the way to the bottom – hanging ready for any climber to come up.

'How does it work from up here though?' said Jack, for the twentieth time. All of them had pulled and twisted and tugged at the ladder, lying so snugly in its hiding-place – but it was quite impossible to move it.

'Give it up!' said Jack gloomily at last. 'No good! We're done for. It's absolutely maddening, just when we are almost out of this beastly mountain.'

20

An amazing secret

They sat in the little room for some time, disappointed and puzzled. Time and again they tried to make the rope-ladder slide out of its secret place, but it wouldn't. In the end they got very thirsty and very hungry. They drank all the water left in the jugs, and wondered where they could get something to eat.

They could only think of the room where they had feasted before. 'Let's go back to it and see if the remains of that meal are still there,' said Jack. 'I could do with another lobster or two!'

'Poor Polly!' remarked Kiki, who always seemed to know when food was being talked about. 'Polly's got a cold. Send for the doctor.'

'Oh, you've found your tongue again, have you?' said Jack. 'I thought you'd lost it! Now don't start screaming or cackling, for goodness' sake, or you'll have us caught!'

They found their way back to the throne-room,

which was still empty, and then to the room where the meal had been.

There were still the remains of the meal there. The children's eyes gleamed. Good! They felt better at once.

They sat down and reached for the food. Then suddenly Jack put his hand on Philip's arm and frowned. A noise had come from the next room – the beautifully furnished bedroom! The children sat as still as mice. Was anybody there?

Kiki suddenly saw Snowy with his front hooves on the table, reaching for the salad. In anger she flew at the kid and screeched.

'That's done it!' said Jack. And as he spoke, the hangings at the entrance to the room opened, and a face peered through.

It was the face they had seen down in the big workroom – the face with the enormous forehead. It had bulging eyes of a curious green-blue, a hooked nose, and sunken cheeks, yellowish in colour.

This face stared in silence at the four children, and they, in turn, stared back without a word. Who was this strange old man with the great forehead?

'Do I know who you are?' asked the face, a puzzled look coming over it. 'I forget, I forget.' The curtains were swung further apart and the old man came right through. He was dressed in a kind of loose tunic of blue silk, and the children thought he looked a pathetic old thing. He had a thin high voice that Kiki immediately copied.

The old man looked astonished, especially as he could not see Kiki, who was behind a great vase of flowers. The children didn't say anything. They were wondering if it was possible to make a dash and get away.

'What are children doing here?' said the old man, in a puzzled tone. 'Have I seen you before? Why are you here?'

'Er – we came to look for somebody who was lost,' said Jack. 'And now we can't get out again. Could you tell us the way?'

The old man seemed so lost and wandering that it seemed to Jack that he might quite well be foolish enough to show them the way out. But he was wrong.

'Oh no, oh no,' said the old fellow at once, a cunning look coming over his yellow face. 'There are secrets here, you know. My secrets. Nobody who comes in may go out – until my experiments are finished. I'm the king of this place – my brain runs it all!'

He finished up on a high shrill note that gave the children an odd feeling. Was the old fellow mad? Surely he couldn't be the 'king' they had seen in the throne-room?

'You don't look like the king,' said Lucy-Ann. 'We saw the king in the throne-room – he was tall and had a great crown, and black hair round his face.'

'Ah, yes. They make me appear like that,' said the old

man. 'I want to be king of the world, you know, the whole world – because of my great brain. I know more than anyone else. Meier says I shall be ruler of the world as soon as my experiments are done. And they are nearly finished, very very nearly!'

'Does Meier dress you up like a king then, when you appear in the throne-room?' asked Jack, astonished. He turned to the others and spoke in an undertone. 'That's to impress the paratroopers, I suppose! He wouldn't cut any ice with them if they saw him like this.'

'I *am* a king,' said the old man, with dignity. 'Because of my great brain, you know. I have a secret and I am using it. You have seen my great laboratory, have you? Ah, my little children, I know how to use all the great powers of the world – the tides, the metals, the winds – and gravitation!'

'What's "Gravitation"?' said Lucy-Ann.

'It is the power that keeps you on the earth – that makes you come back to it when you jump, that brings a ball back when you have thrown it,' said the old man. 'But I – I have conquered gravitation!'

This seemed a lot of nonsense to the children. They were quite sure the poor old man was mad. He might have had a marvellous brain at one time – but he couldn't be much good now.

'You don't believe me?' said the old fellow. 'Well, I have discovered some rays that repel the pull of the earth.

Do you understand that, my children? No, no, it is too difficult for you.'

'It's not,' said Jack, interested. 'What you mean is – you think you've got hold of some rays that, if we use them, will cancel out gravitation? So that if you used the rays, say, on a ball, it wouldn't feel the pull of the earth to bring it back here, but would speed through the air and not fall to earth?'

'Yes, yes – that is it – very very simply,' said the old man. 'And now, you see, I have invented these wings. I send the rays through them. I imprison them in the wings. And then, when a man jumps from an aeroplane, he presses a button to release the power of the rays – and he does not fall to earth! Instead he can glide and soar, flap his wings, and fly like a bird until he tires of it – then he can imprison the rays again and glide to earth!'

The children listened to all this in silence. It was the most extraordinary thing they had ever heard.

'But – is it really true?' asked Lucy-Ann at last. The idea of flying like that was very tempting!

'Do you think we would have come here to this lonely mountain for our experiments, do you think Meier and Erlick would have poured out their money if they had not known I could do this?' demanded the old man, looking rather angry.

'Well – it just sounds so extraordinary, that's all,' said Lucy-Ann. 'It sounds perfectly *lovely*, of course – I mean,

I'd give anything to be able to fly like that. How clever you must be!'

'I have the biggest brain in the world,' said the old man solemnly. 'I am the greatest scientist that ever lived. I can do anything, anything!'

'Could you show us the way out of here?' asked Jack, in an innocent voice. The old man looked uncomfortable.

'If you use my wings, then you can go,' he said at last. 'We are all prisoners here till then, even I! Meier has said this must be so. He says I must hurry, hurry to get my wings quite perfect – time is short. Then I shall be made king of the whole world, and everyone will honour me.'

'Poor old man,' thought Philip. 'He believes everything that rogue of a Meier says. Meier and Erlick are using his brains for their own purposes.'

As suddenly as he had appeared, the old man went. He seemed to forget they were there. He vanished through the curtains and left them alone. They looked at one another, feeling uneasy.

'I don't know how much to believe,' said Jack. 'Has he really got hold of the secret of how to cancel out the pull of gravitation? Do you remember how peculiar we felt when we were looking at that extraordinary brilliant mass down in that pit – we felt sort of light, as if we ought to cling on to the balcony, or we'd float off into the air? Well, I bet some of those rays he spoke of were flying loose then!'

'Gosh, yes – that was strange,' said Philip thoughtfully. 'And, of course, all this would have to be done underground – so that the rays couldn't go flying off everywhere! The heart of a mountain seems a jolly good place for a terrific experiment like this – walls of thick rock all round. No wonder we heard rumblings and felt the earth shaking! That old scientist knows a thing or two. I'd be scared stiff to meddle with all the powers that scientists use nowadays. This is more extraordinary than splitting the atom.'

'I don't understand about things like that,' said Lucy-Ann. 'I feel like the people of old must have felt towards their magicians – I don't understand what they're doing, but it all seems like magic, and I'm scared!'

'You wait till you put on a pair of non-gravitation wings or whatever he calls them,' said Philip, helping himself to a peach. 'That'll be magic if you like.'

'Meier and Erlick must believe in the ideas the old man has,' said Jack. 'Or they wouldn't go to all the terrific trouble they do – and try to keep everything such a secret. I suppose, if the idea really came to something, they'd make such a colossal fortune that they'd be the richest men the world has ever known – and the most powerful.'

'Yes. *They'd* be the rulers – not the old man,' said Philip. 'They're just using him, and stuffing him up with all kinds of stories. He's as simple as can be, though he's got such a brain. They would give out that *they* were the inventors, not the old man. Fancy keeping him a prisoner here like that – and everyone else too!'

'Us included,' said Dinah. 'Well, I'm beginning to see daylight a bit now – understanding what's going on here – but I just can't believe it. Nor will Bill!'

They finished a very good meal. Nobody came to interrupt them. There was no sound from the old man's room. The children thought perhaps he had gone to bed for a rest, or had returned to his weird underground pit. They all made up their minds that nothing would persuade them ever to go down there again!

'What shall we do now?' said Jack. 'Snowy, tell us! Kiki, you've had enough peaches.'

'Poor Polly,' said Kiki sorrowfully, and wiped her beak on the table-cloth.

'Someone's coming!' suddenly said Lucy-Ann. 'Quick, hide!'

'Behind the hangings on the wall,' whispered Dinah, and the four children fled to the loose hangings. They squeezed behind them and waited, holding their breath.

It was two of the soldiers, who had entered the room to clear away the meal. They talked to one another in surprised voices, and indeed, they were filled with astonishment to see so much of the food eaten.

The children heard their light feet pattering to and fro. Then one of them gave a sharp exclamation, which the children didn't understand. They stood behind the curtains, their hearts beating fast. Kiki was on Jack's shoulder, silent and puzzled.

Suddenly Lucy-Ann gave a loud scream, and the two boys leapt out from behind their curtains at once. One of the soldiers had seen her foot below the hangings, and had pounced on her.

'Jack! Philip! Quick, save me!' she cried, and they rushed to her rescue.

21

On the mountain-top

Both the soldiers had got hold of poor Lucy-Ann. She was screaming wildly, and the two boys flew at the men. But to their great surprise they were thrown back as easily as if they had been feather-weights. Just a twist of the men's arms, and back they went, falling headlong to the floor.

They were up again in a trice – but this time one of the soldiers caught Philip in a vicious grip, and the boy found himself turning over in the air, and flying right over the man's head! He landed with a crash on the table, and sent all the dishes into the air.

What with Lucy-Ann's screams, the boys' yells, and the crashes of the dishes there was a terrific commotion. Kiki added to it by screeching loudly. Then she flew down and attacked one of the men. He fended her off.

Four more soldiers suddenly appeared, and that was the end of the children's resistance. They were all captured.

Kiki flew off somewhere, still screeching. Snowy had disappeared completely.

The four children were marched out of the room and taken to a bigger room, well furnished, but not nearly so elaborate as the king's rooms. Hangings covered the walls, but they were plain and simple. The roof of the cave was not covered, and the children could see the rough rock above their heads.

Lucy-Ann was sobbing. Dinah looked very pale and the boys were angry and defiant. They were all stood in a row against the wall. Philip felt in his pocket to see if his slow-worm was hurt in the scuffle. Sally Slithery had not liked life in the mountain. She had become lethargic and dull. But she would not leave Philip.

She was still there, coiled up. Philip wondered where Kiki and Snowy were. It was not like Kiki to fly off like that. She must have been very scared – or perhaps one of the dishes had struck her as it flew off the table.

In a few minutes Meier and Erlick, the two men who were the real power behind the poor old 'king', came into the room. Meier was glowering, and his piercing eyes glanced from one child to another sharply.

'So! There are four of you! Three of you came to find this boy, I suppose – and let him out of the cave he was in. You thought you could all escape – you thought it would be easy, so easy. And it was not?'

He fired this question at them, with a twisted smile on his hawk-like face.

Nobody answered. 'How did you find the way to let down the rope-ladder?' The man fired this question at them so suddenly that they jumped. 'Who told you how to get it down?'

Nobody said a word. Meier's eyes began to narrow, and the girls felt uneasy. He was horrid!

'I asked you a question,' he said. 'You, boy, answer me!'

'I used my brains,' said Jack shortly, seeing Meier looking at him.

'Does anyone else know of that entrance?' said Erlick suddenly. The children looked at him with dislike. He was like an ape, they thought! Meier was bad enough – but Erlick was ten times worse.

'How do we know?' said Philip, beginning to boil at the way these two men spoke to them. 'What does it matter if they do? Is what you're doing here so shameful that you need to hide even the entrance to the mountain?'

Erlick stepped forward and slapped Philip across the face. Lucy-Ann stopped crying, in greater fright than ever. Philip did not flinch. He looked the man boldly in the face, and did not even rub his smarting cheek.

'Leave him alone, Erlick,' said Meier. 'There are better ways of bringing a boy like that to heel than by slapping his face. And now we will send out the dogs to scour the countryside. If these children have friends anywhere near, the dogs will find them, and bring them in.'

The children's hearts sank. Would the Alsatians capture Bill and David then – and bring them to the mountain to make them prisoners too? That would be dreadful.

From somewhere outside came a hollow cough. Meier and Erlick jumped. Meier went to the entrance to the cave and looked out. There was nobody there at all.

'Is there another of you?' asked Meier. 'Is it boy or girl?'

'Neither,' said Jack, who had recognized Kiki's cough, and was hoping she would keep out. It would be just like these men to wring her neck.

'Pooh! Gah!' came Kiki's voice, and then a cackle that was enough to make the men's blood curdle. They went to the entrance of the cave again, and had a good look round, but Kiki was safely perched on a shelf of rock above their heads, and they could not see her at all.

'Send for the doctor,' said Kiki, in a sepulchral voice, that sent shivers down the men's backs. 'Send for the doctor.'

'Good heavens! Who *is* it?' said Erlick. He looked threateningly at the four children. 'If that's another boy out there, being funny, I'll skin him alive!'

'There are only four of us, two boys and two girls,' said Jack.

'And here we all are,' said Philip, in an insolent voice. He knew it was foolish to talk like this to the two men, but he couldn't help it. Both he and Dinah were fool-hardy when their tempers were up.

'Oh! And here you'll all stay!' said Meier. 'And I'll think up something to take the spirit out of you, my boy. You may have gone through your life cheeking everyone and throwing your weight about – but you won't do it with me. Now – walk in front of us, and keep going!'

The children were forced to walk out of the cave in front of the two men. They soon found themselves stumbling up the stone spiral stairs, going up and up. They came to the openings where the stores were, and then went on past those till they came to the door of the cave in which Philip had been bolted.

'Hey, you, boy! You're to go into that cave again,' ordered Meier. 'A few days without much to eat will soon take the insolence out of you. You others go on up.'

Poor Philip! He was shut once more into the cave that looked out to the sky – but this time he had no Sam to keep him company. He sat down, wishing he hadn't been so foolish as to cheek the two grim men. Then he was glad he had. *He* wasn't going to kow-tow to two rogues like that. All the same it was a pity he wasn't with the others – especially as now there was only Jack to be with the girls.

The other three were forced to go on higher, climbing steadily. And then – what a surprise!

They came up a broad flight of steps hewn out of the rock, on to the very top of the mountain itself. They stood there, catching their breath at the sight of the amazing panoramic view all round them. The top of the world! Surely they must be touching the sky itself!

The three forgot their troubles for a moment as they gazed round in wonder. Everywhere they looked there were mountains, rising high. Valleys, deep in shadow, lay far far below. It was wonderful to be up there in the blazing sunshine and cool breeze, after being in the dark mountain for so long.

The top of the mountain was extraordinarily flat. On three sides rose steep rocks, like teeth. Jack knew in a flash what mountain it was – Fang Mountain, the one he had noticed when they had set out. He looked round the mountain-top. Nothing grew there at all. It was bare, flat rock, the size of a great courtyard. At one side, playing cards in the shade, were the paratroopers.

They stared in surprise at the children. Runaway Sam was with them and he pointed to Jack and was evidently telling his companions about him and the others. Jack was glad that Philip had told Sam so little about himself and the other three. He did not want Meier to know any more than he already did.

There was an awning rigged up on the side opposite the paratroopers. Meier pushed the children towards it.

'You will stay here,' he said. 'You will not talk to those men over there at all. You will not go near them. You are prisoners, you understand? You have forced your way in here, where you are not wanted, and now we shall keep you here as long as we wish.'

'Can't Philip come with us?' begged Lucy-Ann. 'He'll be so lonely away from us.'

'Is that the other boy? No. He needs a little punishment,' said Meier. 'A little starvation diet! Then we will see if he will talk civilly.'

Meier and Erlick then left the three and disappeared into the mountain again. Jack and the girls sat down, looking doleful. Things weren't too good! It was a thousand pities that poor Philip was apart from them.

Evidently the paratroopers had been warned that they were not to go near the children, for they made no attempt even to shout to them. It was obvious that Meier and Erlick were used to being obeyed.

There was a natural parapet of rock near where the children were, that ran round the edge of the mountain just there. Jack got up and went to it. He sat on it and put his field-glasses to his eyes. If only he could spot Bill! And yet he was afraid that if Bill was there anywhere, the dogs might set on him and find him. He wondered where all the dogs were.

Then he sat up a little straighter on the parapet and focused the glasses on a small spot on the slope of the mountain. He had seen a movement. Could it be Bill and David and the donkeys?

No, it wasn't. It was the dogs! They had evidently already been let loose and were ranging the countryside.

If Bill was anywhere about, they would soon find him! Blow! Then Bill would be captured too. Jack wished he knew some way of preventing this happening, but he couldn't think of anything.

He wondered about poor old Dapple. Thank goodness they had tied him up so very loosely. He had plenty of range, and there was grass and water for him. But how the donkey would wonder what had happened to everyone!

Something touched Jack's hand and he jumped and looked down. It was Snowy! The kid had found his way to them and was nuzzling Jack in a half-scared manner.

'Hallo, Snowy! Have you been looking for Philip?' said Jack, rubbing the kid's soft nose. 'He's in that cave again. You can't get to him.'

Snowy knew that very well. He had already been to bleat outside Philip's door. He looked so dismal that Jack took him to the girls and they all made a fuss of him.

'What do you suppose has happened to Kiki?' asked Lucy-Ann after a time.

'Oh, she'll turn up all right,' said Jack. 'She knows how to take care of herself. Trust Kiki for that! She's probably leading those two men a fine old dance, coughing and sneezing and cackling and making a noise like an express train screeching in a tunnel!'

Jack was perfectly right. Kiki had been playing a fine game with Meier and Erlick, and as they had no idea that the children had a parrot, they were two extremely puzzled men. A voice without a body to it – how very strange!

Nothing happened for some time. Then, when the sun was sinking, there came a clamour of howls and barks, and the pack of Alsatians was brought up to the top of the mountain by two of the soldiers. The children watched to see if Bill had been caught, but there was no sign of any prisoner with the dogs. They heaved a sigh of relief.

The dogs were taken to a big wire enclosure some way off the children. 'You be careful of dogs,' said one of the guards to the children. 'They bite hard. You be careful!'

22

The helicopter

The children, however, were not in the least afraid of the dogs, for had they not all slept together with them some nights before? They did not tell this to the soldiers, of course. They waited till the men had disappeared and then they went over to the dogs.

But Philip was not there this time, and the dogs did not feel the same towards the girls and Jack as they had done towards Philip. They growled when Jack came near to them, and one showed his enormous white teeth. Lucy-Ann and Dinah shrank back.

'Oh! How terribly fierce they look! They've quite forgotten us. Jack, be careful.'

Jack was not afraid, but he was cautious when he saw that the dogs did not want to be friendly. They were strong, fierce creatures, disappointed in their hunting that day, hungry, and suspicious of Jack. Now, if he had been Philip how different their behaviour would have been! Philip's magic touch with animals would have put everything right. He had an irresistible attraction for all live creatures.

'Come away from them,' said Lucy-Ann, when she heard the growling taken up by most of the pack. 'They're making a perfectly horrible noise – just like wolves would, I'm sure.'

They went back to their own part of the mountain. 'A corner for the dogs, a corner for us, a corner for the men!' said Jack. 'Well – I wonder how long we're going to be here!'

Nobody brought them anything to eat at all for the rest of that day. They thought it was a very good thing they had had such good meals in the king's room! Jack wondered if they were supposed to lie on the bare rock to sleep. What brutes those men were, if they meant to keep them without rugs or food!

But just as it was getting dark three of the soldiers appeared. They carried rugs with them, which they threw down at the children's feet. One had brought a pitcher of water and mugs.

'What about something to eat?' asked Jack.

'Not bring,' said one of the men. 'Master say not bring.'

'Your master not nice,' Jack told him. 'Your master very nasty.'

The men said nothing. He and the others went away, soft-footed as cats. The children curled up in their rugs, wondering how Philip was faring, alone in his cave.

The next morning was unbelievably beautiful when the sun rose and lighted up the mountain-tops one by one. The three children sat on the parapet and watched. They all felt very hungry indeed. Snowy was with them. Kiki had still not appeared and Jack was getting a little worried about her.

Snowy leapt up on to the parapet beside Jack. There was a very steep drop from there, with a tiny ledge of rock jutting out some way below. Nobody could escape by climbing down, that was certain. He would just go slipping and sliding down the mountain and break all his limbs in no time.

Snowy stood there, his little ears pricked up as if he was listening. He suddenly bleated very loudly. And then, very muffled, hardly to be heard, a voice answered. Jack leapt up from the parapet. Was it Philip's voice? Where was his cave then? Anywhere near where they were?

Lucy-Ann and Dinah joined Jack, seeing his sudden excitement. Then Snowy gave them a really terrible shock. He jumped right over the mountain-top, off his perch on the parapet of rock!

'Oh!' shouted Lucy-Ann. 'He'll be killed!'

She wouldn't look to see what happened, but Dinah and Jack watched in horror. The little kid had leapt to the tiny ledge of rock jutting out some way below the parapet. He landed on it with all four tiny hooves close together! There was only just room for them – not half an inch to spare!

He stood balanced there, and then, when it looked as if surely he must topple off, he leapt to a small ledge lower down, slithered down a rough bit, and disappeared completely.

'Goodness gracious! What a thing to do!' said Dinah, taking a deep breath. 'My heart almost stopped beating.'

'Is Snowy all right?' asked Lucy-Ann, still not daring to look.

'Apparently. Anyway he's disappeared – and I should think he's probably found the cave where Philip is,' said Jack. 'All I hope is he won't try to get back the same way – or he'll certainly break his neck.'

But Snowy did get back the same way and appeared on the parapet about half an hour later, looking as frisky as a squirrel.

And round his neck was a note! It was tied there with string. Jack took it off quickly and opened it. He read it to the others.

How are you getting on? I'm all right except that I've nothing to eat, and only water to drink. I believe those brutes are going to starve me out! Can you send Snowy with anything for me to eat when you get a meal?
Cheerio!
Philip

At that moment the guards arrived with a meal for the children. It was all out of tins but there was plenty. With it was a loaf of fresh bread. Dinah said she thought perhaps the soldiers had an oven down in the pit somewhere to bake their bread.

They waited till the men had gone and then Jack debated how to send food to Philip. He made some sandwiches and wrapped them up firmly in the paper the soldiers had brought the bread in. He slipped a note inside the sandwiches to say they would send food by Snowy whenever they could. Then he tied the packet very firmly on to Snowy's back. Snowy smelt it and tried to reach it, but he couldn't.

'Now you go to Philip again,' said Jack and patted the parapet to show Snowy that he wanted him up there. As soon as he was up Snowy remembered Philip and down he went again on his clever little feet, landing on first one tiny ledge and then another.

The other three felt pleased to think that Philip was having a meal instead of being starved. Jack took a look round the countryside below with his field-glasses, as they sat and ate, wondering if Bill would come that day. Time was getting on now. Surely Bill would arrive soon!

The day passed very slowly. The paratroopers were taken off into the mountain by the soldiers and didn't come back. The dogs were also taken out and Jack was sure he could see them ranging the countryside again.

They sent food to Philip by Snowy each time they

had a meal. It was a help to exchange cheery notes with him even though nobody felt all that cheerful. Kiki hadn't yet returned and all the children were now very worried about her.

The evening came. The paratroopers had not come back and the children wondered why. The dogs came back, however, but this time the children did not go over to them. The Alsatians were fighting over their meat and sounded savage and fierce.

It was a cloudy, sultry evening. The children dragged their rugs out from under the awning to a place where the breeze blew more strongly. They lay down, trying to go to sleep. The two girls slept, but Jack lay wide awake, feeling worried about Kiki and Philip and the girls too.

He heard a noise far away in the distance and sat up. He knew what that was – it was a helicopter! There was no mistaking the noise now. Was it coming to the mountain?

He awoke the two girls. 'Dinah! Lucy-Ann! The helicopter's coming. Wake up and let's watch. Get back under the awning, in case it lands too near us.'

The girls dragged their rugs under the awning. They went to sit on the parapet and listened, wondering if Philip was awake and listening too. He was. He was lying on his tummy, looking out of his cave, watching and listening. It was too dark for him to see anything much, but he hoped he might share in the excitement.

The noise came nearer and at last sounded very loud.

'Look – there it is,' said Jack, excited. 'See – going round the mountain a bit above us. Aren't they going to flash a light here to show it where to land?'

As he spoke two of the soldiers appeared in a hurry on top of the mountain. They ran to the middle of the great rocky courtyard and did something the children could not see. Immediately a strong light flashed upwards into the sky, and in its beam the children saw the helicopter, its wheels poised almost above their heads.

'There it is! It's landing!' cried Jack. 'See how it's dropping down slowly, almost vertically! It's just the right sort of machine to land on a mountain-top!'

The helicopter came down to the courtyard and stopped. The vanes ceased to whirl above it. Voices hailed one another.

'It's a jolly *big* helicopter,' said Jack. 'I've never seen such a big one before. It must be able to carry quite a large cargo.'

The beam of light was now directed on the helicopter and the children could see what was going on quite clearly. Boxes and crates were being tumbled out of it on to the ground, and the hard-working men were all very busy handling them, dragging them about, opening some of them and taking the contents down the stone steps to the store-places.

A lean-faced young man with a scar right across his cheek was the pilot of the helicopter. With him was a swarthy fellow who limped badly. They spoke to the workers in curt tones, and then left their machine and disappeared into the mountain.

'Gone to report to Meier and Erlick, I should think,' said Jack. 'Come on – let's go and have a look at the helicopter. Wish I knew how to fly it! We could escape nicely in it now.'

'And hover outside Philip's cave and take him off too!' said Dinah. They all went over to the machine. Jack got into the pilot's seat and felt grand. How he wished he knew how to fly the helicopter!

He was still sitting there when Meier, Erlick, the pilot and his companion, and one of the paratroopers appeared. Jack tried to scramble out before he was seen but he was too late. Meier saw him and dragged him out so roughly that he fell to the ground.

'What are you doing? You keep away from this machine!' shouted Meier in a fury. Jack skipped off to the girls, rubbing his shoulder.

'Are you hurt, Jack?' asked Lucy-Ann anxiously. He whispered that he was all right. Then he said something that made the girls stare fearfully at the group of men in the centre of the courtyard.

'I believe that paratrooper is the next one to try those "wings". They've brought him up to show him the helicopter and where he's to jump from.'

Both the girls thought it would be dreadful to have to leap from a machine high up in the air – and trust to the king's extraordinary 'wings'. They wondered how many people had tried them and failed. Nobody would know if they were efficient or not until they had been tried.

The paratrooper looked the helicopter over thoroughly. He talked to the pilot, who answered him shortly. Jack thought that the pilot wasn't any too keen about the para-jumping part. He would probably have been content to fly the goods to the mountain and finish at that.

'Tomorrow night you leave,' said the voice of Meier, cutting through the night. 'Come and eat now.'

Leaving two soldiers to guard the helicopter from the curiosity of the children, the rest of them disappeared into the mountain. Tomorrow night! What would they see then?

23

The wonderful wings

The three children retired to their rugs. They were afraid to go near the helicopter again, because the obedient soldiers, they knew, would stand no nonsense. Snowy appeared from over the parapet, full of curiosity. He ran over to the helicopter, but the guards hit out at him.

'The beasts! How can they be cruel to a little kid?' said Jack. 'Snowy! Come here! These fellows would make you into soup as soon as look at you. You'd better be careful.'

'Oh, Jack – don't say things like that,' said tender-hearted Lucy-Ann. 'Would they really? Surely nobody would ever have the heart to hurt Snowy?'

Snowy retreated hastily to the children and skipped up and down the parapet, as sure-footed in the dark as in the daylight. The beam of the lamp showed up the helicopter, but the rest of the courtyard was in darkness.

The dogs howled in their enclosure. They had not liked the noise the helicopter made, and they were uneasy and restless. The soldiers shouted threateningly to them, but the dogs took no notice.

'I don't like this adventure at *all*,' said Lucy-Ann suddenly. 'In fact, I simply hate it. I want to get away. I want to go back to Bill and Aunt Allie and Effans and Mrs Evans. Why did we have to find another adventure in these nice, peaceful summer holidays?'

'It just happens to us,' said Jack. 'Something in us attracts them, I suppose – like animals are attracted to Philip! Some people attract good luck, some attract wealth, some attract animals, some attract adventures.'

'Well, I'd rather attract something harmless, like cats or dogs,' complained Lucy-Ann. 'Oh dear! I do wish Snowy wouldn't keep walking over us when we're lying down.'

They fell asleep at last. In the morning, when they sent some food to Philip by Snowy, they sent a note also, telling him all they had seen in the night. Snowy brought a note back.

I'm sorry for the paratrooper! I wonder how many they've used in trying out this mad experiment. I'm glad I'm not chosen for anything as crazy as that! Keep your chin up! I'm all right here. I've got Snowy most of the time and Sally Slithery is getting so tame she eats out of my fingers. She sleeps on a bit of warm rock at the edge of my cave. Tell Snowy not to tread on her when he comes bounding in!
So long!
Philip

The day seemed very long again. The dogs were not taken down into the mountain and let loose on the countryside, but were exercised round and round the courtyard by the diligent soldiers. The children were glad about that.

'If old Bill arrives today, the dogs won't be out on the mountain-side. He'll be safe. So let's hope he comes. Not that he can do much if he does. He won't know where the entrance is – and if he finds it, he won't know how to work the rope-ladder – and there's no other way of getting in.'

Lucy-Ann looked very dismal. 'Shall we have to stay here all our lives long?' she asked.

The others laughed at her. 'No!' said Jack. 'Bill will do *some*thing – but don't ask me what!'

The paratroopers had not appeared again that day, not even the one who was supposed to be going to use the 'wings' that night. The helicopter stood there in the middle of the courtyard, the sun glinting on its motionless shape.

Evening came. The children grew restive. The soldiers had brought them food as usual, but had not said a word. What were all the paratroopers doing? Having a ceremonial feast of something to celebrate their comrade's experiment?

And where, oh where, was Kiki? Jack was feeling very miserable about her now. He turned over and over in his mind all the things that might have happened to her. She had never been away from him so long.

That night the beam shone out again in the court-yard. Meier, Erlick, three or four servants and the paratrooper appeared, followed by the lean-faced, scarred pilot and his companion.

Then up the opening, stepping out majestically, came the king!

He was dressed in his grand robes and crown and was hardly recognizable as the poor, bald old fellow who had talked to the children a day or two back. He held him-self proudly as he walked to the centre of the courtyard.

Behind came four uniformed guards, carrying a box. They laid it down at the king's feet. In silence he stooped down and opened it.

He took out a pair of wings! They glittered like gold, and were shaped like a bird's outstretched wings, big and wide. Lucy-Ann gasped in delight.

'Oh! Look, Dinah! Real wings! Aren't they lovely?'

The king was speaking to the amazed paratrooper. 'These will hold you up when you jump. Press this but-ton here as soon as you leap from the helicopter. Then you will find that you cannot fall. You will no longer feel the pull of the earth. You will be free and light as air. Then you may use the wings, for guiding yourself, for planing, for soaring, whatever you wish!'

'Doesn't it sound marvellous?' whispered Lucy-Ann, drinking in every word.

'The wings must be fitted to your arms,' said the king. 'Hold them out and I will fix them on.'

'Here – is this all I'm going to have to stop me falling?' said the paratrooper.

'You will not need anything else,' said the king. 'In these wings are imprisoned powerful rays. At the press of the button they are released, and shoot towards the earth, preventing its pull on you. You cannot fall! But when you want to come to earth, press the button once more – and you will glide down gently, as the earth exerts her pull on you once more.'

'Yes, but look here – I understood it was a new kind of parachute I was trying out,' said the paratrooper. 'See? I didn't think it was stuff and nonsense like this!'

'It is not nonsense, man,' said Meier's curt voice. 'It is a great invention by the greatest scientist in the world. You will find Erlick and me waiting for you to come to earth when you have flown a mile or two. We shall take the dogs and find you. Then – riches for you, and honour for the rest of your life! One of the pioneer flying-men!'

'Look here – I'm a heavy chap,' began the paratrooper again. 'See? Those flimsy wings won't hold *me* – rays or no rays! I don't know about any pull of the earth on me – all I know is I'll have to fall, once I jump out with only those things on my arms. Are you crazy?'

'Get him!' suddenly said Meier, in a furious voice. Erlick and the soldiers at once pinioned the paratrooper's arms. He had to stand whilst the king fixed on the 'wings'. The children watched with bated breath.

The paratrooper cried out and struggled, but the ape-like Erlick was far too strong for him. 'Put him in the helicopter and take off,' commanded Meier. 'Go too, Erlick. Push him out at the right moment. If he's a fool he'll not press the button. If he is wise he will press it – and then he will see how well he flies!'

But the pilot now had something to say. He spoke in a drawling voice, clear and contemptuous.

'I think this fellow's too heavy. The last one was too. You'd better think again, boss, and get those wings made twice the size. I'm game for an experiment where there's a chance for everybody – but I reckon there's not much chance for a big fellow trying out those wings of yours.'

'Do you mean you refuse to take this fellow?' said Meier, white with anger.

'You've got it right first time, boss,' said the pilot, getting angry too, so that his scar showed up very plainly. 'Try a little fellow! I guess the experiment worked all right last time – for a minute or two – and then it petered out. These paratroopers are hulking great chaps – the ones you try out with me, anyway – and I tell you plainly I'm not taking anyone who doesn't want to go. Got it?'

Meier went up to the pilot as if he meant to strike him. Erlick pulled him back. 'That's right,' said the pilot, who had not turned a hair. 'Don't try any funny business with me, boss. I know too much – and there's others will know too much too, if I don't get back on time!'

He got into his machine, and the swarthy man, his companion, who had not said a single word all this time, got in beside him. The paratrooper watched them dazedly. The engine of the helicopter started up.

The pilot leaned forward and spoke again to Meier, who looked as if he was on the point of bursting with rage.

'So long! I shan't be coming next time – I'm going for a holiday! I'll be sending somebody who's not so pernickety as I am – but I warn you – try a little guy!'

The machine rose vertically into the air, circled round the mountain-side slowly, and then made off to the west. In a few minutes it could not even be heard.

The children had watched all this, the girls only half understanding what was going on. Lucy-Ann felt sorry for the frightened paratrooper and very glad he had not been forced to go off in the helicopter.

The little group left in the courtyard paced up and down. A lot of talk and argument went on, though the paratrooper did not seem to be joining in at all. He had stripped off the wings and was held securely by the soldiers. The king carried his precious wings all the time, but at last replaced them in the box and locked it.

'Very well,' he said, 'I agree. It may be that the men we choose are too heavy – but who else could we have asked? Only paratroopers are used to jumping from heights! Try someone lighter if you wish. It will make no difference to my ideas.'

And then the children heard a few words that made them gasp in horror. 'One of those kids will do,' said Meier. 'That insolent boy, for instance. We'll put the wings on him and he shall jump from the helicopter!'

24

The helicopter comes again

When the courtyard was completely empty, and the beam had gone out, leaving the mountain-top in darkness, Lucy-Ann began to cry bitterly. Jack and Dinah put their arms round her. They felt like howling too.

'He doesn't mean it,' said Jack, trying to think of something really comforting. 'Don't worry! He only said that to scare us. They'd never make Philip do a thing like that.'

'They didn't say it to scare us. They meant it, you know they did!' sobbed Lucy-Ann. 'What are we going to do? We've got to do *some*thing.'

It was all very well to say that – but what in the world was there to do? The children got very little sleep that night. They debated whether to tell Philip or not what had happened – and what was proposed.

They decided not to. It would be dreadful for him to lie alone in his cave and worry. So, when morning came and they sent Snowy to Philip with the usual sandwiches made from their own breakfast rations, they said nothing in the daily note about what had happened.

But to their great surprise, who should be ushered up the steps by the soldiers that morning, but Philip himself! He bounded forward to greet them, grinning.

'Hallo! They've let me out! Tired of starving me, I suppose, and seeing me get fatter and fatter. I say, did you see the helicopter last night? I heard it.'

Lucy-Ann and Dinah hugged him and Jack slapped him heartily on the shoulder. They were delighted to see him again. Snowy had come with him and acted like a mad thing, careering up and down the parapet as if he was in a circus.

They told him very little about the night before. He was rather puzzled that they said so little, even in answer to his questions. But Jack, by means of heavy frowns, had let the girls know they had better not say too much. He thought it would be wise to postpone saying anything in case Meier really hadn't meant what he said.

But it looked a bit odd, Meier letting Philip come up to be with the others, all of a sudden – and bringing them very much better food and plenty of it. 'Like victims being fattened for the sacrifice!' thought Jack. 'I wonder when the next helicopter's due? How long have we got? Oh, Bill, do make haste!'

Lucy-Ann and Dinah, fearing that poor Philip really would have to jump from the helicopter, were most affectionate to him. Dinah even enquired after Sally the slow-worm and did not shrink away when Philip brought her out of his pocket.

'I say! What's up with Dinah?' asked Philip at last. 'She's gone all sweet and sugary. It's not like her. She'll be offering to nurse Sally Slithery for me next!'

Philip felt sure there was something up. He couldn't *imagine* what it was. He wondered if it was bad news about Kiki. No – if Jack had heard any, he would be much more upset than he was. Philip felt uncomfortable. It wasn't like the others to keep anything from him. He tackled Jack about it firmly.

'Look here, Jack – something's up. Don't say there isn't – I jolly well know there is. So come out with it – or I'll go back to my cave and sulk!'

Jack hesitated. Then he took the plunge. 'All right, Philip – I'll tell you. But it's not good.'

He told him all about it – how the helicopter had arrived – what had happened – about the frightened paratrooper and the angry pilot – and finally about Meier's wicked suggestion that one of the children should try the 'wings'.

'I see,' said Philip slowly. 'And I suppose the one they're going to try is me?'

'That's what they said,' said Jack. 'The brutes! That experiment is only half-way to perfection – the wings aren't a hundred per cent foolproof, nor even fifty per cent – though they may be one day!'

'Well, well – to think I'm going to fly with wings,'

said Philip, trying to pass the whole thing off as a joke. He saw Jack's troubled face. 'Don't worry, old son. It won't happen! Something will turn up – and if it doesn't, I'm no coward!'

'I know. You don't need to tell me that,' said Jack. 'The girls are awfully upset. That's why we've seemed a bit funny with you. We just didn't want to tell you.'

Philip pranced up to the girls, flapping his arms like wings. 'Cheer up!' he cried. 'As soon as I'm out of that helicopter I'll fly off to Bill and give him the shock of his life!'

But it wasn't much use trying to make a joke of it. It was too serious. None of the children felt like playing with Snowy, who was very hurt and gambolled down the stone steps into the mountain to look for somebody with a bit more fun in them.

Three days went by. The children had almost given up all hope of Bill coming now. Surely he would have been along before, if he had come looking for them? They would have seen a search-party on the mountain-side, if one had come. But they saw nothing at all. It was most disappointing. They felt quite sick with watching and waiting.

They pondered whether to make a dash for freedom again and try for the rope-ladder once more. But Jack shook his head. 'No, they'll be on the watch now. There's always one of those soft-footed soldiers about. Meier will have put somebody on guard.'

There was one good thing, orders had evidently been given to feed the children well, and they had plenty of good food. Even their sad hearts did not take away their appetites and they tucked in well, helped by Snowy, who would devour every scrap of greenstuff or vegetable if he could.

And then, one night as they slept together under the awning, their rugs pulled round them, they heard the familiar sound of the helicopter! All four sat up at once, their hearts beating. Tears came into Lucy-Ann's eyes.

The helicopter circled round the moutain-top slowly. Then the bright beam came on and the courtyard was lighted up. The helicopter came slowly down and at last its wheels rested on the rocky yard.

There were two men in the machine, but neither of them was the same as before. The pilot had on big goggles and a peaked cap. The other man was bare-headed. He looked stern and grim.

Meier soon came up with Erlick and the soldier guards. 'You the boss?' called the pilot. 'I've taken Kahn's place. He's on holiday. Had a job finding this place. This is Johns, my mate. We've got the goods you wanted.'

There was the same unpacking as before, and boxes and crates were piled on the ground. The pilot and his companion jumped down.

'There is a meal ready for you,' said Meier. 'You will start back tomorrow night?'

'No. Got to leave tonight,' said the pilot. 'They're

making enquiries about some of our doings. Got to be back at once.'

'You have been told that – er – that er . . .' began Meier.

'What – that some paratrooper wants a jump off the helicopter?' said the pilot. 'Oh, yes. That's okay by me. If a chap wants to do that, well, it's no business of mine.'

'You will be paid very very well,' said Meier's grim voice. 'This time it is double the price. We have a young jumper – it is necessary for our experiments, you understand.'

There was a pause. Then the pilot's voice came again, sharp and enquiring. 'What do you mean – a *young* jumper?'

'A boy,' said Meier. 'He is here.' Then he turned to one of the soldiers and said something to him in a foreign language. The soldier darted off down the steps into the mountain. 'I have sent to tell the inventor that you have arrived,' he said. 'Now will you come to have a meal?'

'No,' said the pilot. 'I must be off. Get this boy and make him ready.'

Lucy-Ann's knees were shaking so much that she couldn't stand. Philip felt calm but rather fierce. All right! Let them strap those wings on him then – let them take him in the helicopter! He'd jump out all right! And if those wings *did* act – *if* they did – but would they?

Philip just couldn't bring himself to believe that they would.

The pilot had not seen any of the children, but now Philip had to go forward, fetched by one of the soldiers. The others followed, though Lucy-Ann had to hold on to Jack. Before the pilot could say a word to them, the king appeared. The children thought he must have dressed himself up very quickly! His crown was a little crooked, but otherwise he looked as majestic as ever.

The box with the wings in was carried by one of the soldiers. The king undid it and took out the wings. They really did look beautiful – and what was more, they looked as if they *would* be able to fly! Lucy-Ann hoped fervently that they could.

Philip made no fuss at all as the wings were strapped to his arms. He was shown the two buttons and nodded. He flapped his arms a little and was surprised to feel the power in the wings, as they met the air. The others watched him in admiration. Jack warmed to him. What pluck he had! – he didn't in the least show that he was scared. Perhaps he wasn't.

But deep down inside Philip was a nasty little core of dread. He kept it clamped down. Not for worlds would he have let anyone know it was there.

Then Meier, the king, Erlick and the others got a surprise. Little Lucy-Ann stepped forward and laid her hand on the arm of the king.

'Your Majesty! I think *I* ought to try out your wings

for you. I am much lighter than Philip. It would be an honour for me to try them.'

Philip and Jack looked thunderstruck. The idea of it! Philip gave the little girl a hug, putting his winged arms all round her.

'You're a brave darling! But *I'm* going! And what's more I'll fly back to this old mountain-top and just show you how well I'm doing.'

Lucy-Ann gave a sob. This was too much for her altogether. The pilot said nothing but got into the helicopter with his companion.

The king showed no hesitation at all in letting Philip go. It was pathetic the way he believed whole-heartedly in his extraordinary wings. His head was in the clouds. The people who performed his experiments for him and tried out his clever ideas were nothing to him at all.

Meier watched grimly as Philip climbed into the helicopter, helped by one of the soldiers, for his arms were hampered by the beautiful wings. The man would have been better pleased if the boy had objected and made a scene. He did not admire Philip's pluck in the least. His piercing eyes looked into Philip's and the boy looked back at him mockingly.

'So long!' he said, and raised one of his winged arms. 'See you later! Look out for youself, Meier. You'll come to a bad end one of these days!'

Meier stepped forward angrily, but the helicopter's engine began to whirr. The rotors went slowly round, gathering speed. Lucy-Ann tried to stifle a sob. She felt sure she would never see Philip again.

The helicopter rose straight up into the air. The pilot leaned forward and shouted something loudly. 'Don't forget Bill Smugs!' he called, and his voice was no longer the same as it had sounded before. It was quite different. It was somebody else's.

In fact – it was BILL'S VOICE!

25

A thrilling night

Only Lucy-Ann, Jack and Dinah knew what the last shout meant. Meier and the others had no idea at all. They hardly heard what was shouted.

But the children had heard all right! They gasped. Jack's hand found Lucy-Ann's and Dinah squeezed Jack's arm. They didn't say a single word until Meier, Erlick, the king and the servants had all disappeared once more. Then they made their way to their awnings, linking hands to keep together.

'Jack! That was *Bill*! Bill himself!' said Lucy-Ann, her voice going all funny as she spoke.

'Yes. And he knew if he yelled out, "Don't forget Bill Smugs," that we'd know it was him,' said Dinah. 'He called himself Bill Smugs the very first adventure we had – do you remember? Gosh – I never had such a surprise in my life!'

'And Philip's safe,' said Jack, in intense satisfaction. 'That's one good thing. The other fellow with Bill must be one of his friends. Philip will just chuck those wings overboard and that'll be that.'

'I feel as if I simply must sit down at once,' said Lucy-Ann. 'My legs will hardly carry me. I feel so joyful!'

She sat down and the others followed suit. They all let out a terrific sigh of relief. A heavy load rolled away from them. Philip was safe! He didn't have to jump out of the helicopter to try out an experiment for a mad old scientist, or for Meier and Erlick. He was with Bill.

'What made Bill think of getting a helicopter?' wondered Jack. 'Landing on the mountain-top with it too – under the noses of Meier and Erlick.'

'Well, don't you remember, you put in your note something about the helicopter we thought was landing up here?' said Dinah. 'The note we left with Dapple.'

'Yes, so I did,' said Jack. 'Well, that looks rather as if old Bill did come along here then – and found Dapple. Good for him! Trust Bill to get going somehow!'

'What's he going to do next?' said Dinah. 'Do you think he'll come back for us?'

'You bet he will!' said Jack. 'He'll park Philip somewhere safe and he'll be back as soon as he can. Perhaps tonight!'

'Oh, how lovely!' sighed Lucy-Ann. 'I don't like this mountain. I like Mrs Evans' farmhouse best. I don't like anyone here – that horrid Meier, and that awful fat Erlick, and those nasty little pussy-footing soldiers – and the king.'

'Well – I feel sorry for him,' said Jack. 'He's just got into the hands of rogues. No doubt they've made plenty of money already from his inventions. Now they're going all out for this one. I do wonder if there's anything in it.'

'Well, I'm jolly glad Philip hasn't got to find out!' said Dinah. 'Good old Philip – he was as plucky as could be, wasn't he?'

'Yes. And Lucy-Ann was jolly brave too,' said Jack. 'Whatever made you think of trying to go in Philip's place, Lucy-Ann?'

'I don't know. It sort of came over me all at once,' Lucy-Ann tried to explain. 'But I wasn't brave. My legs were wobbling like jelly.'

'The only thing that worries me is Kiki,' said Jack. 'I hope those men haven't done anything to her. She's never been away from us so long. I haven't heard so much as a hiccup from her!'

The others were worried too. Dinah couldn't help feeling pretty certain that Kiki had come to some harm. If Meier caught her that would be the end of her. Dinah shivered when she thought of his cold, piercing eyes.

Suddenly she gave a small shriek. 'Oh! Something's wriggling over my leg! What is it, quick?'

'It's the slow-worm,' said Jack, making a grab at it. 'Sorry, Dinah. You see, Philip didn't want to make poor old Sally share his jump – so he slipped her into my pocket when he thought you weren't looking. I didn't know she'd got out. Don't yell, Dinah. With everybody

218

being so frightfully brave tonight, you might as well show your pluck too!'

And, surprisingly, Dinah did. After all, what was a slow-worm compared to Philip's jump – if he had had to jump? Nothing at all. Dinah drew her leg away, but made no fuss at all. Sally slithered round them for a little while and then went into Jack's pocket again.

'I just simply can't get over knowing it was Bill in that helicopter!' said Lucy-Ann for the twentieth time. 'My heart jumped nearly out of my body when he suddenly changed his voice to his own and yelled out, "Don't forget Bill Smugs!"'

'We'll have to be on the look-out for when he comes back,' said Jack. 'I'm sure it will be tonight. Perhaps no one will hear him but us, because we'll be the only ones expecting him. You can't hear a thing down in that mountain.'

'Oooh – wouldn't that be super, if Bill came back without being heard, and took us off?' said Lucy-Ann. 'What *would* Meier and the others think! They'd hunt all over the place for us!'

'And send the dogs out too,' said Jack.

'Shall we keep awake to look out for him?' said Dinah.

'No, you girls have a nap. I'll keep watch,' said Jack. 'I'm much too wide awake to go to sleep. I'll wake you as soon as ever I hear anything.'

'What about that beam of light that shows the

helicopter where to land at night?' said Dinah suddenly. 'Can you turn it on when you hear it coming, Jack?'

'I expect so,' said Jack, and went into the middle of the courtyard to find the switch that turned on the powerful beam.

But he couldn't find it anywhere. He hunted all over the place and gave it up at last. 'Can't find where the wretched thing turns on,' he said. 'Sickening!'

'Well, I daresay Bill can land all right,' said Lucy-Ann, who had the utmost faith in Bill's ability to do anything, no matter how impossible. 'You keep watch, Jack. I'm going to have a nap.'

She and Dinah shut their eyes, and in spite of all the terrific excitement of that night, they were both asleep in half a minute. Jack sat up, keeping watch. It was a cloudy night, and only occasionally did he see a star peeping out from between the clouds.

Good old Bill! How had he got that helicopter? How did he know how to fly one? Jack felt very thankful indeed that they had had the sense to leave a note behind with Dapple, telling everything they knew. Otherwise Bill wouldn't have known a thing about the mountain or its secret, and certainly wouldn't have guessed that helicopters landed on the top!

From far away a noise came through the night. Jack strained his ears. Yes – it was the helicopter coming back. It hadn't been long then – just long enough to drop Philip somewhere, hear his story and come back for the others. What a sell for Meier to find them all gone – and not to know what had happened to the wonderful wings!

The boy went to try and put on the lamp again, but could not find the switch at all. This was not surprising, because it was set in a tiny trap-door, let into the yard.

The helicopter came nearer. It circled the mountain. It rose vertically to land on the courtyard. Jack shook the two girls.

'It's here! Bill's back!'

The girls woke up at once. Snowy, who was asleep by then, woke up and leapt to his feet. He could feel the terrific excitement of the others, and sprang about madly.

'Look – it's landing!' said Jack, and the three of them strained their eyes to see the helicopter, a big dark shadow in the blackness of the night.

There came a slight crashing sound, and then the heli-copter suddenly swung over to where Jack and the girls were. They had to dodge out of the way.

Bill's voice came on the air. 'Jack! Are you there?'

Jack ran to the helicopter as Bill switched on a pow-erful torch. 'I'm here, Bill. The coast's clear. Nobody's up here. Gosh, it's good to have you! Is Philip all right?'

'Quite all right. He's down on the mountain-side with Johns, the fellow who came with me, waiting for us. Get into the helicopter, all of you, and we'll go while the going's good.' Bill switched his torch round to see where the girls were, and in a moment all three were being helped up into the machine.

'I couldn't quite see where to land,' said Bill. 'I must have hit something coming down. I felt a good old jolt, and the helicopter swung round like mad. I hope she's all right!'

'You went into part of the rocky parapet, I think,' said Jack, helping the girls in. 'Oh *Bill*! This is grand! How did you . . .'

'All explanations later!' said Bill, and began to fiddle about with something in front of him. 'Now – here we go!'

The helicopter rose a foot or two in the air and then swung round in a peculiar way. Bill put her back to earth again at once. 'Now what's wrong? She shouldn't do that.'

Lucy-Ann was so longing to be off that she could hardly bear this. 'Let's go, let's go,' she kept saying, till Dinah nudged her to stop. Snowy was on Lucy-Ann's knee, as good as gold. She held on to him tightly, tense with excitement.

Bill tried again. Once more the machine rose into the air, and then did its peculiar swing-round. 'Something's wrong with the steering,' said Bill, in an exasperated voice. 'Why did I leave Johns down there? He might have been able to put it right. But I didn't think this machine would hold him as well as you three!'

In deepening dismay the children sat whilst poor Bill

tried his best to get the helicopter to rise and fly properly. But each time it swung round violently, and Bill could do nothing with it. He was secretly rather afraid that it would get completely out of control and swing right off the mountain-top. He could not risk an accident with the three children on board.

For at least an hour Bill experimented with the steering of the helicopter, but it would not answer to the controls at all. He made the children get out to see if lightening the load made any difference, but it didn't.

'It must have got damaged when you struck the parapet,' said Jack. 'Oh, Bill – what are we going to do now?'

'What about the way out by the wall?' said Bill. 'Philip told me all about it – something about a rope-ladder and so on. As a matter of fact, I did go to find the entrance there, when I came to look for you the other day – you spoke of it in your note, you remember – and I went behind the green curtain, found the crack in the rock and went in. But I couldn't go any further than that curious cave with no roof and the black pool at the bottom.'

'No. Nobody would find how to get out of that cave except by accident,' said Jack. 'We discovered how to get the rope-ladder down from above – by turning a wheel under the water in the pool. Down came the ladder!'

'Well – it seems to me we'll have to try to get out that way,' said Bill. 'This pest of a helicopter won't answer to her controls now. I daren't try and take off. We'd crash – and we haven't any wonderful wings to save us, either!'

'Oh, Bill – can't we really fly off in the helicopter?' said Lucy-Ann, her heart sinking like lead. 'Oh, I don't want to go down into that horrid mountain again! We might lose our way. We might get caught!'

'We'll have to try, I'm afraid, Lucy-Ann,' said Bill. 'Never mind – I'm here to protect you now. And, after all, it's the middle of the night, and nobody is likely to be about.'

'If only that helicopter would go properly!' said Jack. 'It's a piece of real bad luck that it won't. It's such a giveaway too. As soon as anyone sees it, they'll know something's up and will come to look for us.'

'All the more reason why we should get a move on now,' said Bill. 'Come on. Gosh, what's this banging against me? Oh, it's you, Snowy. Well, if you come too, you'll have to keep at our heels or you'll give the game away! By the way – where's Kiki? I haven't seen or heard her tonight.'

'We don't know *where* she is,' said Jack miserably. 'We haven't seen her for days – not since we were captured. She may be caged somewhere – or hiding in the mountain – or even killed!'

'Oh, *no*!' said Lucy-Ann. 'Don't say that. Kiki's too clever to let herself be captured. Perhaps we'll find her tonight!'

'Where's the way out of this place?' asked Bill, switching on his torch. 'Over there? Are there steps that go down into the mountain? Well, come on then. Every minute is precious now.'

They left the damaged helicopter in the yard and went towards the stone steps that led down into the mountain. Lucy-Ann shivered.

'I hoped I'd not go down there again! Take my hand, Bill, I don't like this!'

26

Flight through the mountain

Soon they were right down inside the mountain. They had passed Philip's cave, passed by the stores, and gone down the steep spiral stairway, cut in the rock.

It was very difficult to choose the right way to go, because all the dim lamps that lighted the passages were out. It was quite dark everywhere. Bill's powerful torch sent a bright ray in front of them, but he had to use it cautiously in case someone saw the light, and was warned of their coming.

There was a lot of standing still and listening, a good deal of argument on Jack's part and Dinah's about the right way to go. Bill was very patient, but his voice was urgent as he told them to think hard and choose the right way.

'If we followed Snowy, we'd probably go right,' said Lucy-Ann at last. 'He would know the way.'

'Well – but he doesn't know where we want to go,' said Jack. 'I mean, if he knew we wanted to go to the rope-ladder cave, he could lead us there all right – but we can't make him understand that.'

They ended up being completely lost. They found themselves in a dark tunnel, with a very high roof that none of the children recognized at all.

Bill began to feel desperate. If only he had been able to land without damage, this long trek through dark, unknown passages wouldn't have been necessary.

They went down very deep, and, quite suddenly, came out on to the high gallery that overlooked the pit. Bill drew in his breath sharply when he saw the mass of brilliance suddenly showing when the curious floor slid back for a moment. He and the children felt the strange feeling of lightness at once, but it passed immediately the floor slid over the glowing mass again.

There was nobody in the pit. Apparently the floor worked automatically by machinery of some kind, though there was none to be seen. That was the curious thing about the works in the mountain – there was no heavy machinery anywhere. Whatever power was used was not conveyed by iron or steel machines, and there was little noise except for the heavy rumbling that sounded before the shaking of the earth.

'There's obviously some metal in this mountain that can be used for that fellow's experiments,' said Bill. 'Some rare metal or other – like uranium, which is used for splitting the atom. There are a few mountains in the world which contain various rare metals – but usually they are mined for it and the stuff is taken out. In this case they haven't mined it – they are using it where it is! It's possible that they have to do that – in order to use the enormous thickness of the rocks in the mountain to protect the outer world from whatever rays they are experimenting with. Very ingenious!'

'I think we know the way back now,' said Jack, quite thankful at having found some place they recognized, even though it was the frightening pit!

He pointed behind them, up the wide, uphill passage that he knew went up and up for a long way. Bill switched his torch on it. 'Is that the way?' he said. 'Well, come along then.'

They went up the wide, steep passage. They came to the narrow, twisty little tunnel they had been in before and walked along till they came to the fork.

'Left-hand fork,' said Jack, and they took that. Bill was amazed to see the beautiful silken hangings that decorated the walls further on, and hung across the entrance to a cave.

Jack put his hand on Bill's arm. 'That's the king's bedroom, beyond,' he whispered. 'Dinah, have you got Snowy? Don't let him rush on in front.'

Bill tiptoed to the curtains and parted them. A dim light shone beyond. Bill looked with interest into the king's bedroom – and then closed the curtains quickly. He tiptoed back to the children.

'There's somebody lying on the couch there,' he whispered. 'An old fellow with a colossal forehead.'

'That's the king of the mountain!' whispered back Jack. 'The Great Brain behind all these inventions. I think he is an absolute genius, but quite mad.'

'He seems to be asleep,' said Bill. 'Is there any way we can go round this cave without waking him up?'

'No. I don't know of any,' said Jack. 'We've got to go through it, and then through a cave where he eats his meals, and then into the throne-room.'

Bill thought for a moment. 'We'll have to risk it then,' he said. 'We'll go through the room one by one, but for heaven's sake don't make a sound!'

They went through the king's bedroom one at a time, hardly daring to breathe. Dinah had tight hold of Snowy, praying that he wouldn't bleat when he went through the room!

Fortunately there were very thick carpets on the floor, so it was easy to make no sound. Lucy-Ann's heart beat so loudly as she tiptoed across that she thought it must surely wake the king with a jump.

Then they were in the room where the long table had held so much lovely food. But now it was empty and there was not so much as a dish of fruit on it.

Then on to the throne-room – and outside this, behind the lovely hangings patterned with the red dragons, the little company paused. A curious noise came to their ears – was it snoring? What was it?

Bill peeped through the hangings very cautiously. He grinned. In the throne-room, sitting or lying, were the paratroopers. A very long table had been set down the middle, and on it were the remains of a lavish supply of food and drink. Not a single man was awake!

'So that's where those fellows have been the last day or two!' whispered Jack. 'I wondered where they were. Gosh, they've fallen asleep where they are – what a pretty sight!'

Bill fumbled about in the hangings they were looking through. He was looking for a switch. He found one and whispered to the children. 'Now listen – I'm going to switch off the light so that we can get through the hall without being seen. Keep close to one side of it and get through as quietly as possible. Even if we do make a noise and some of those fellows wake up it won't matter – because they won't be able to see who it is!'

This was a good idea. The light went out with a slight click and the great hall was in darkness. The children, led by Bill, moved quietly along one side, their feet making no noise on the soft mats.

When they came to the immense laboratory Bill stood still in amazement. He knew a great deal more about these things than the children did, of course, and he could see what a brilliant, ingenious mind must be at the back of all the things at work there.

They stood in the gallery and looked down at the

wires and wheels, the glass jars and the crystal boxes, and heard the quiet, purposeful humming going on.

'What is it all doing, Bill?' whispered Lucy-Ann.

'It's transmuting, or changing, one power or energy into another,' said Bill soberly. 'Making it into usable form, so that . . .'

'So that it can be imprisoned in those "wings", for instance?' said Jack.

'Something like that,' said Bill. 'It's an amazing set-up altogether.'

There was nobody there. It did seem extraordinary that all these humming, spinning, whirring things should go on and on seemingly of their own accord, with just the king wandering round them occasionally.

Bill was so fascinated that for a few moments he forgot the urgency of finding the way out of the mountain. There was something dream-like about all this – it didn't seem real.

He was brought back to reality again by feeling Snowy butting against him. He jumped a little. Then he took Lucy-Ann's arm. 'Come along! What am I thinking of, stopping like this!'

Jack had found the passage that led out of the laboratory. He led them down it and they came to the great cave they had seen before. Bill's torch swept round it but there was nothing to see. Then they went into the passage that led to the roofless cave! The children felt they really were getting near freedom again – if only, only,

only they could find out how to get that rope-ladder out of its place in the wall!

They passed the dim lamps, which, for some reason or other, were lighted here. They came to the roofless cave, and Bill's torch picked out the pitchers of ice-cold water standing at the back to refresh those who had had the long and exhausting climb up the rope-ladder.

'This is the place where the ladder's kept,' said Jack, and he took Bill's torch and swung it to find the place in the rocky wall where they had seen it last.

But before he could spot it, Lucy-Ann tripped over something and fell with a thud. Bill picked her up. She had hurt her knees but she didn't make a sound. Bill told Jack to flash his torch on Lucy-Ann to see what she had fallen over.

She had stumbled over the rope-ladder itself! There it lay, stretching from its place in the wall, over the floor and then disappearing downwards over the edge of the cave – down, down, down to the cave with the pool far below!

'Look! The ladder's out!' cried Jack, forgetting to whisper in his excitement. 'Oh, Bill – let's come on down at once!'

'Somebody must have gone out of the mountain tonight,' said Dinah, 'and left the ladder down to come back by. I wonder who it was. We'd better be careful we don't meet them!'

'Jack, you go down first,' said Bill, who had been

examining with great interest the way the ladder was attached to the hole in the wall. It was extremely ingenious. Bill could see how wires must be run up from the wheel in the pool to a lever which released the ladder – whose weight then compelled it to run out over the floor to the edge of the cave, where it fell and then pulled itself undone until it had come to its last rung. What made it able to roll itself up again Bill could not imagine – but the brain that could devise all the amazing things inside that mountain would find that a very simple problem!

Jack went to the place where the ladder hung over the edge. He knelt down and put his feet one after another on a rung a little way down. The ladder felt as firm as before. It was very well made and strong.

'Well, here I go,' said Jack. 'Send the girls next, Bill, and then you come. Snowy's gone already, down whatever little hole he and the dogs use! I don't know where that is. I only wish I knew where poor old Kiki was. I don't like leaving her all alone in this beastly mountain.'

Bill shone his torch on him. The girls watched his head disappear as he climbed down.

'You go now, Lucy-Ann,' said Bill. 'Jack must be a good way down. You won't tread on his head. Then Dinah can go, and I'll follow last of all. Don't attempt to leave the cave below till I am down with you.'

Jack was going steadily down. What a long long way it was! And then a very peculiar thing happened. The ladder began to shake below him! Jack stopped climbing at once.

'Gracious! Somebody's climbing *up*! And I'm climbing down! Whoever can it be!'

27

Escape at last

No sooner had he felt certain that somebody was climbing up very steadily below him than Jack immediately stopped climbing down and began climbing back again at top speed. He didn't want to meet Meier or Erlick on that ladder.

Some way up he bumped into Lucy-Ann's feet. She gave a small squeal of surprise. 'It's all right, Lucy-Ann. It's only me,' said Jack in a low voice. 'There's somebody coming *up* the ladder. Go back again as quickly as you can!'

Lucy-Ann at once began to climb up as fast as possible, in a great fright. Gracious! How awful to feel that somebody was coming up the ladder just as they were going down! She felt certain it was that horrid Meier!

She in turn bumped into Dinah's feet and passed the urgent message on to the surprised girl. Dinah began to climb back again up to the cave at the top very quickly indeed. Lucy-Ann and Jack were immediately below her.

Jack felt as if somebody might catch his ankles at any moment.

And, of course, the next thing was that Dinah nearly got her head trodden on by Bill's big feet. He was descending at top speed to join the others, and was most amazed to find Dinah just below him.

'What's the matter? Didn't I tell you to buck up?' he said, and then caught Dinah's agonized whisper.

'Somebody's coming up! Quick, before they get Jack. Quick, Bill!'

Muttering something under his breath, Bill climbed back quickly. He pulled Dinah up, then Lucy-Ann, then Jack. The ladder still shook. The climber, or climbers, were coming up steadily.

'Back into the passages!' commanded Bill. 'We can't afford to be caught now. We'll wait till whoever it is has gone and then we'll try again.'

They came to where the passage forked into three, and Bill pushed them all up into the darkest one – but coming towards them were footsteps, and somebody's shadow at the far end! They all rushed back again.

But now the climber had reached the top of the ladder and was behind them. They tried the second passage and found themselves in a maze of funny little caves, all leading one out of another.

'Wait here!' said Bill. But they had been seen, and challenging voices now began to echo along the dark passages.

'Who's there? Come out at once!'

They didn't stir. They were all crouched in a dark corner, overhung by a rocky ledge. Bill wondered if the beam of a torch would find them. He was afraid it would.

The feet passed by in another cave. Then came more voices. The hunt was on! Bill groaned. It sounded as if four or five searchers were about now. They would separate and search until they had found them. And they had been so near freedom!

'Come,' said Bill after a moment. 'We'll try a better cave than this.'

But, before they could move, the flash of a torch shone into their cave. They all stiffened and stood absolutely still. The beam came nearer and nearer. Lucy-Ann forgot to breathe, and stood with her hand firmly clasped in Bill's.

Just as the beam of the torch was picking out Jack's feet – or so it seemed to Jack – a surprising interruption came. A voice came from somewhere near by, a hollow, mournful voice, full of misery and despair.

'Poor Kiki! Ding dong bell! Peepbo!'

Jack's heart leapt. *Kiki!* She wasn't dead, then! She must have been wandering, completely lost, all about the passages and caves for days. She didn't know they were close to her. She had seen the light of the torch and heard voices, and as usual she had joined in the conversation.

Bill's hand squeezed Jack's arm warningly. He was

afraid the boy might call Kiki, or exclaim out loud in delight. But Jack held his tongue. Kiki went on talking in the most melancholy voice imaginable.

'Send for the doctor! Musty, fusty, dusty, pooh, gah!'

Jack had never heard her so miserable before. Poor Kiki! She must have thought herself quite deserted.

A sharp voice rang through the cave. 'What in the world was that? Somebody's in this cave! Erlick, come here! Did you hear that?'

'What?' asked Erlick, coming in with another torch.

'A voice,' said Meier. 'Somebody's in here. Two people, probably. One talking to another. Stand there with your torch whilst I walk all round with mine.'

Meier began to walk round, examining all the walls carefully for hiding-places. Bill groaned silently. Now they had no chance to get to another cave at all.

Kiki gave a realistic sneeze and then a cough. Meier stopped his search and swung his torch in the direction of the sound.

'We can hear you! Come out or it will be the worse for you!' he shouted, in a furious tone.

Kiki was frightened. She had been without food for some time, and was hungry and unhappy. The man's angry voice filled her with panic and she flew off into the next cave, having no idea that her beloved Jack was so near her. It was just as well that she didn't know, for if she had known she would certainly have flown to Jack's shoulder and given their hiding-place away at once!

Her voice came from the cave further on.

'Polly put the kettle on! Send for the doctor!' Then came a loud hiccup, and an apologetic 'Pardon!'

'Good heavens! What's going on?' cried Meier, completely puzzled. 'It's that voice again that we've been hearing at intervals. Well, where there's a voice there's a body and I'm going to find it this time, if I have to shoot the caves to pieces!'

A loud report made Bill and the children jump in fright. Meier had drawn his revolver and fired wildly in the direction of Kiki's voice. Jack didn't like that a bit. He was afraid Kiki might be hit.

Meier and Erlick went into the next cave after Kiki's voice. It came to them from further away.

'Upsadaisy! Wipe your feet, you naughty boy.'

The children couldn't help smiling, scared though they were. Kiki always managed to say such ridiculous things in moments of urgency. There came another shot, which echoed all round the caves.

Kiki gave a cackle of scornful laughter, and then made a noise like a car changing gear. She came back to the next cave again, and the men followed. They still had not caught sight of Kiki because they were looking for a human being, running away in front of them, whereas Kiki flew high in the roof of the caves, and perched on small ledges, well hidden.

Somebody else ran through the cave where the children were, calling to Meier.

'Mr Meier, sir, sir! All children run away! Helicopter come back. All alone on mountain-top. No one there. Children run away!'

It was one of the numerous soldiers, who had evidently discovered the returned helicopter, and the disappearance of the pilot and the children. There was an amazed silence.

Meier raised his voice and let forth a stream of furious foreign words, none of which Bill or the children could understand. Then came Erlick's voice.

'No good going on like that, Meier. Get out the dogs. The children must have gone down the ladder. You left it down when you went out tonight, didn't you? The dogs will soon round them all up.'

'What's happened to the pilot, though?' raged Meier, and lapsed into some foreign language again. The soldier came pattering back through the cave again, presumably on his way to get the dogs.

'Send for the doctor,' called Kiki mournfully. She screeched like an engine and made Meier flash his torch in and out of the caves again, almost beside himself with rage.

Erlick, Meier and one or two others with them then began a loud argument in many languages. Bill didn't wait to hear what it was all about. He pushed the children out of their hiding-place and towards the nearest passage. Very quietly and quickly they all fled back towards the cave with the ladder. Maybe there was a chance now of escape. Jack wished with all his heart that he could take Kiki too.

They went down the ladder in the same order as before, Jack wondering fearfully if he would find anyone coming up this time, ready to catch him by the ankles. But he didn't. He reached the bottom safely, his legs shaking with the effort, panting and exhausted.

Lucy-Ann almost fell off the last rung, weak with relief to find she was at last at the bottom. It had seemed an endless climb down to her. She sank to the ground beside the pool, her heart beating painfully.

Dinah followed and threw herself on the ground too. Then came Bill, not so distressed as the others, but very glad indeed to be at the bottom of the ladder.

'Phew! The bottom at last!' he said. 'What a climb! Now come on – out we go on the mountain-side. We'll join up with Philip and Johns. If only those wretched dogs don't find us! Philip's told me about them and how you thought they were wolves. I don't fancy a pack of Alsatians on my trail, somehow, with Meier and Erlick urging them on!'

The dawn was beginning to come over the mountains. The sun was not yet above them, but a golden light was spreading upwards from the east. The children were very glad indeed to feel the fresh wind on their faces when they went out through the crack in the rock, and swung aside the big green curtain of creeper and bramble. They took deep breaths and gazed around them in the silvery light of dawn.

'Come on,' said Bill. 'I left Philip and Johns by a stream – where you left Dapple. We took Dapple back with us by the way, when David, Effans and I came with the rest of the donkeys to look for you. Philip said you'd know where the place was, even if we landed a little way from it in the helicopter – he thinks we're all coming through the air of course, to land on a good flat place where we left a light burning to guide me. It was a bit tricky landing in the dark with Philip and Johns! The helicopter nearly overbalanced. Still, we managed it.'

'Philip will be looking out for us by that light then?' said Lucy-Ann. 'Not by the stream.'

'No. I told him not to, in case anyone was roaming about there, saw the light and spotted him and Johns,' explained Bill. 'I thought Meier and Co. might possibly be on the look-out for Philip, if they thought he had jumped. I was supposed to radio back to them what had happened – but I didn't, of course!'

It was easy to find their way to the meeting-place, now that dawn was coming. But before they got there, a bit of good luck came to Jack – in the shape of Kiki!

She suddenly sailed down on him from the air with a cackle of delight, and a screech that nearly deafened them all. She flew to his shoulder and rubbed her head into his ear, giving it little pecks and pulls of love. Jack was so overjoyed that he couldn't say a word. He just scratched Kiki's head and made funny, loving noises, which Kiki immediately copied.

'Oh, *good*!' said Lucy-Ann in delight. 'Oh, Jack! Dear old Kiki, isn't it lovely to have her again. It's been awful without you, Kiki.'

Even Bill joined in the demonstrations of affection. 'You saved us, Kiki, old bird! You led those fellows such a song and dance that they let us escape. How did you know where we were? Did you fly out and follow us?'

Kiki didn't tell them, so they never knew, but Jack felt sure she had flown down into the roofless cave, and come out of the crack into the open air. Then she must have heard their voices and come to join them.

'God save the Queen,' said Kiki, in a happy voice, and gave a loud hiccup. 'Pardon! Pardon the queen pop goes Polly!'

'Oh, Kiki! We thought you were dead,' said Dinah. She looked round, missing Snowy. 'And now Snowy's gone! Where is he?'

'He hasn't been with us for some time,' said Bill. 'He'll turn up, I expect – just like Kiki!'

'Dithery Slithery,' said Kiki suddenly, cocking her head on one side and looking at Jack's pocket. Sally the slow-worm was half in and half out, enjoying being out in the fresh air again. Dinah didn't even squeal!

They went on their way, with Kiki firmly on Jack's shoulder – and suddenly they heard a yell.

'Hie! Here we are! Jack! Dinah! Lucy-Ann! Bill! And

oh, I say, there's Kiki too. Hurrah! You've escaped! But where's the helicopter? We've been waiting and waiting for it.'

It was Philip, of course, leaping up and down like a mad thing, with Johns standing stolidly behind him – and Snowy frisking about round them both. He had found Philip! So all the family were together again. They were full of delight – but wait – what was that howling noise in the distance?

'The dogs!' said Jack. 'They're after us!'

28

Trailed by the dogs

Lucy-Ann shrank back against Bill and Johns when she heard the savage howls and barks. She didn't at all like the idea of the dogs being after them!

Bill and Johns exchanged glances, and Bill said something under his breath and looked stubborn and angry. They had all been so pleased at their escape – and now here they were, about to be caught again! Nobody could do anything against ten man-hunting dogs!

'Bill! Get into the stream and wade up through the water,' said Jack suddenly. 'That's what the other man did when he wanted to break his scent. Dogs can't smell a trail through water. Let's all wade up the stream, and try and find a good hiding-place – a big tree, like Sam went up.'

'Well – it's a poor chance,' said Bill, 'but we'll try it! Blow that helicopter – behaving like that just when I wanted to take off to safety! We'd have been quite all right by now if it hadn't been for the damage to the steering.'

They all waded into the middle of the little stream. Up it they went, the water very cold to their feet. Lucy-Ann was between Bill and Johns. She felt very glad indeed that there were two grown-ups with them! In the distance the dogs barked again. They were certainly on the trail!

The little company went up the stream as quickly as they could, so that their scent was well broken. But they could easily be seen, and it was essential that they should get up into a tree, or find a cave as soon as they could.

And soon they found just exactly the thing! The stream disappeared into a large hole in the mountain. The clear water came bubbling out from there into the sunshine, swirling round the feet of the two men and the children – and of Snowy too!

'Look – it comes from that big hole,' said Bill, pleased. 'We'll go in there and hope it will take us all. We ought to be able to hide here till the dogs give up all hope of finding us.'

They crawled in one by one. Bill switched on his torch. There was only just room for them all, because a few yards back the hole narrowed down to a tiny tunnel, out of which the stream gushed madly.

They sat down where they could, squeezed up closely against one another. Jack and Philip had their feet in the stream. They sat there, listening to the distant yelping of the Alsatians.

Bill pulled some chocolate out of his pocket. 'I forgot about this,' he said, and handed it round. It was very comforting to have something to nibble. Johns had brought some too, so there was plenty.

'Do you think the dogs have lost the trail now?' asked Jack, not hearing the barking coming any closer.

'Yes. Sounds like it,' said Bill. 'They're at a loss, I should think. They must have come to the stream, jumped over it and found the trail was at an end. They probably won't have the sense to realize we've gone upstream.'

'But I should think the men with them would guess,' said big stolid Johns, who was taking this extraordinary adventure with the utmost calm, as if things like that happened to him every day. 'I know I would! If I were hunting a man with dogs, and we came to a stop by a stream, I'd order the dogs up- or downstream at once.'

'Oh dear!' said Lucy-Ann. 'Would you really? Well, I'm sure Meier will, then, when he catches up with the dogs, because he's terribly clever. He's got the most piercing eyes, Bill – honestly, they go right through you.'

'Well, he'd better not try looking right through *me*,' said Bill. 'He'd be sorry!'

'Pardon!' said Kiki. 'Sorry!'

'You forgot your hiccup, old thing,' said Jack, and Kiki solemnly produced one. Johns laughed suddenly.

He said he'd heard plenty of hiccups without birds, and seen plenty of birds without hiccups – but when you got the two together it was worth a lot!

'The dogs are coming nearer,' said Jack suddenly. They all listened, straining their ears. It was true. Their howls were distinctly louder.

'Meier's caught up with them, then,' said Dinah. 'And he's guessed our trick, and they're all coming upstream.'

'Yes. And they're sure to smell us here,' said Philip. 'Absolutely certain to. We can't diddle dogs like that!'

'Hey diddle diddle,' said Kiki, and screeched.

'Shut up,' said Jack, and tapped her on her beak. 'Do you want the dogs to hear you?'

'Pooh,' said Kiki, and nipped Jack's ear.

'Listen! I can hear the dogs splashing in the stream!' cried Philip. And so he could. The sound came to everyone's ears, and Lucy-Ann clutched Bill's hand even more tightly. Would this horrid adventure never end?

And then they saw the first dog, his red tongue hanging out, his breath coming in excited pants. He was half leaping in the water, not wading – in and out he leapt, in and out, coming nearer and nearer.

Then came Meier's hateful voice. 'Go on! Get them! Find them!'

The leading dog came right up to the hiding-place. He could smell everyone in there, as he stood in the stream outside the hole. He did not attempt to go in. He had found what he had been told to find – he had not been told to capture and hold.

He lifted his head and howled like a wolf. Kiki was very surprised. She attempted an imitation but an Alsatian's howl was beyond her. She only produced a curious whirring noise that made the dog cock his big head on one side and listen.

Then the other dogs came up, panting too, their tongues all hanging out. They stood beside and behind their leader, sniffing. They looked very fierce indeed!

'Not a nice sight,' murmured Bill to Johns, who was staring stolidly at the dogs as if he was perfectly used to being hunted by a pack of Alsatians and didn't mind it at all.

'Keep still,' Bill commanded everyone. 'As long as we don't attempt to move or get away, the dogs won't do anything more than stand there and stare.'

There came the sound of shouts and Meier and Erlick appeared, very red in the face with running. Meier stopped dead when he saw the pack of dogs standing looking in the hole where the stream poured out.

He pushed Erlick behind a tree quickly. It was plain that he feared Bill might have a gun. He shouted out loudly.

'Come on out! The dogs have found you. If you don't want them to set on you, come on out – and throw any gun you've got down on the ground, and put your hands up. We've got you covered.'

'Pleasant fellow, isn't he?' said Johns to Bill. 'It'll be nice to get hold of him. Do we go out, boss, or don't we?'

'We don't,' said Bill shortly. 'I doubt if he'll dare to set the dogs on us. He knows the children are here.'

'Meier wouldn't stick at anything,' said Jack. And he was right. When there was no answer, and not even a movement from the hole in the hill, Meier began to lose his temper as usual. He shouted out something in a foreign language, then changed to English.

'You heard what I said. You have one more chance. The dogs are ready to pounce. They'll round you up all right, and I warn you, their teeth are sharp, so don't resist!'

Still nobody moved. Lucy-Ann shut her eyes. She really couldn't look at the eager, panting dogs any more. She could see that they were just awaiting the word to rush into the cave and drag them all out.

And then Philip suddenly moved, and before anyone could stop him, he was outside the cave.

'Put your hands up!' called Meier, and Philip put them up. The dogs sniffed at him, and under his breath Philip talked to them.

'Don't you remember me? I'm Philip. You slept with me up on the rock. Fine dogs you are. We're friends, don't you remember?'

The dogs did not understand one word, but they understood his tone of voice. They remembered this boy. They felt his friendliness and his attraction. The leader began to whine a little. He longed to have this boy pat his head. But Philip had his hands above his head, and had only his voice to charm the dogs with.

He went on talking to them in a low voice, whilst the other children, and Bill and Johns, watched spellbound. They all thought the same. Philip, Philip, what is there in you that makes all creatures your friends? What gift have you got, so rare, so irresistible? 'Lucky boy!' thought Bill. 'And lucky for every one of us that you can charm these dogs!'

Meier called out angrily. 'Where are the others? Tell them to come too, or I'll give the order for them to be dragged out!'

The leader dog stood up and put his paws on Philip's shoulders. He licked the boy's face. It was a very wet lick, but Philip did not even turn away his face. That was the signal for all the other dogs to come round too. Quite forgetting Meier, they milled round Philip, trying to get near him, sniffing at him, giving him a lick when they got near enough.

He put down his hands. Meier would not dare to take a shot at him now in case he killed a dog! He ran his hands over their backs, patted their heads, rubbed their noses, and all the time he talked to them in the special voice he kept for animals.

Meier snapped out an order to the dogs. 'Fetch them out! Get them! Bring them here!'

The dogs turned their heads automatically at his commanding voice. They hesitated. The leader looked at Philip. 'Come with me,' said Philip. 'Come. You will find more friends in here.'

And, to Meier's everlasting astonishment, the boy actually led all the dogs to the cave, where at least four of them squeezed in to lick Lucy-Ann, Jack and Dinah! They sniffed doubtfully at Bill and Johns, growled at Snowy and Kiki, and then, when Philip laid a hand on Bill's arm and then on Johns', they accepted them as friends too.

'Philip! You're a marvel!' said Bill, in heartfelt admiration. 'It's magic you use – can't be anything else!'

'What a boy!' said the stolid Johns, allowing his face to change its expression for once in a while, and show great admiration.

'Meier's shortly going to have a fit, I think,' said Jack. 'He just can't understand all this!'

'Fetch them out, I say! I'll shoot the lot of you dogs, if you don't obey orders!' stormed Meier. 'What's come over you? Fetch them out!'

The dogs took absolutely no notice at all. Their leader had accepted Philip as master now, and they all followed his decision. What Philip said they would obey. They feared Meier, but they loved Philip.

Meier suddenly fired his revolver in a fury. He did not fire at the dogs, but over their heads. They jumped and growled, turning their heads towards him. Bill judged it was time to do something.

'Philip! Will the dogs obey you? Will they go for Meier and Erlick? If they will – order them to! We'll give that couple a taste of their own medicine!'

29

The tables are turned!

'Right!' said Philip. He pointed to the tree where Meier and Erlick were hiding behind its big trunk. 'See, boys! Fetch them out! Bring them here! Fetch them for me, then!'

Before Meier or Erlick knew what was happening the pack of Alsatians was speeding joyfully to obey. The whole pack flung themselves on the two rogues, and bore them to the ground. There was no chance to use a revolver. In fact Meier's gun rolled on the ground and was completely lost under the scrambling crowd of dogs.

'Don't hurt them! Bring them here!' ordered Philip in excitement, proud of his power to give commands to the pack of dogs.

Bill and Johns were now out of the cave, and Jack followed. The girls did not come out yet. They didn't want to! Lucy-Ann clutched Dinah's arm till she squealed. Both girls watched what was happening, breathless with intense excitement.

The dogs began to drag the two men over to Philip. Erlick, the great ape-like fellow, a real bully if ever there was one, was screaming for mercy, a coward, like all bullies. 'Call them off! I'll surrender! Call them off, boy!'

Meier fought savagely, not seeming to care whether he was bitten or not. He could not find his revolver and was beside himself with amazement, anger and fear.

The dogs were trained not to bite unless commanded, but one or two of them gave him a well-deserved nip – a little repayment for his callousness in dealing with them in their training. The leader got hold of him by the slack of his trousers, and, looking rather ridiculous, Meier was brought to where the boys and the two men were standing watching.

Then Erlick was brought too, trying to stand, almost weeping with panic. He remembered a gun he had in his pocket, and he reached to get it, thinking it was his last chance of escape.

But Johns was on the spot. 'Hands up,' he said. 'Any funny business on your part, Erlick, and the dogs can have you for all I care. Stand up, Meier, and put your hands up too.'

White with rage Meier put up his hands when the dogs allowed him to find his feet. He glared at the boys and Bill.

'What did you do to the dogs?' he snapped at Philip. 'They've never turned on me before!' He lapsed into a foreign language again and poured out streams of abuse.

'Shut up,' said Bill, who was now holding his own revolver in his hand. 'You talk too much.'

'Wipe your feet,' said Kiki's voice and she flew out of the hole and on to Jack's shoulder. 'Pooh! Gah!'

Meier glared at the parrot, recognizing the voice that had puzzled him for so long. If looks could have killed, certainly Kiki would have fallen dead at that moment. As it was she went off into one of her dreadful cackles, and Meier clenched the fists he was holding above his head, wishing that for one moment he could get hold of Kiki.

'What do we do now?' enquired Jack. 'It's a long way from home, Bill – and we've got no food to keep us going if we have to walk back.'

'Effans and Trefor and David are not far off,' said Bill. 'I told them to stand by somewhere near this mountain with plenty of donkeys, in case we needed them. I wasn't sure if the helicopter would fly very far with such a lot of you on board!'

'*Oh!* Will they really be near here?' said Lucy-Ann, gladly. 'Oh, Bill – you think of everything! Oh, *good*!'

'Can we take the dogs back with us?' asked Philip, who was still surrounded by furry bodies and wagging tails. 'I could look after them till we get them away somewhere. I daresay you'd like them for the police force, Bill. They're jolly well trained.'

'Thanks for the offer,' said Bill, with a grin. 'I'll accept it. And now – quick march! We'll leave this surprising mountain behind, and I and a few others will come back to it later. I feel it wants a little cleaning up. And we'll take that mad genius in charge before he does something dangerous. I wouldn't put it past him to blow up the mountain.'

'Good gracious!' said Lucy-Ann, in alarm. 'Well, let's get away before he does!'

They set off at a smart walk. Meier and Erlick walked in sullen silence. They had their hands by their sides now, for Johns had searched them both, and they were now weaponless. Jack and the others began to feel a familiar feeling of emptiness under their belts.

'I'm jolly hungry,' announced Dinah. 'Has Effans brought any food with him, do you think?'

'Well, Mrs Evans was so upset to hear that you were lost, that she immediately did an enormous baking,' said Bill, 'and I believe two of the donkeys are laden with the results. So let's hurry!'

'Where are they?' asked Jack.

'In the Vale of Butterflies, waiting for us patiently,' said Bill, with a grin. This was a most surprising thing to hear.

'The Vale of Butterflies!' cried Jack. 'Why, we couldn't find it! We began to think it was all Trefor's make-up!'

'Oh, no. It was really quite easy to find, if only David had known how to read a map,' said Bill. 'The name was on it in Welsh, so you wouldn't have understood it. But I don't believe David has ever learned to read a map properly! I shouldn't have let him go off with you as guide.'

'Did *you* find it then?' asked Lucy-Ann.

'Oh, yes. It's on the way here, actually,' said Bill. 'David took a wrong road, that's all – accidentally left the track. Anyway I told him to wait there with the donkeys, because I thought you'd rather like to see the butterfly valley, after having missed it and found a very strange mountain instead!'

'Oh! Everything's coming right!' said Lucy-Ann joyfully. 'The adventure is over, isn't it, Bill? Well – it doesn't seem nearly so bad now as it did!'

'Poor Lucy-Ann!' said Bill. 'You do have adventures thrust upon you, don't you? Never mind, you'll soon be back at the farm, enjoying Mrs Evans' wonderful cooking!'

'As soon as you came, things were all right,' said Lucy-Ann happily. 'It was super hearing you yell out, "Don't forget Bill Smugs!" last night. Gosh, was it only last night? It seems years ago!'

They went through a narrow pass between two mountains, feeling hungrier and hungrier – and there below them was the Vale of Butterflies!

They stopped in delight. The valley was a froth of coloured butterflies, red, yellow, white, pink, blue, copper, brown! There were thousands there, fluttering in the sunlight, darting erratically to and fro, hovering, dropping down to the millions of flowers. These made a carpet of brilliant colour, and the children thought they had never seen such a lovely sight before.

'Why are there so many butterflies, I wonder!' marvelled Dinah.

'I suppose because there are so many varieties of food-plants,' said Bill. 'This valley is apparently as famous for flowers as for butterflies, but because it is so much off the beaten track, it is rarely visited. I've no doubt the pack of dogs would have kept trippers away, anyhow!'

'There's Effans – and the donkeys!' cried Philip. 'Hey, Effans! Hallo, Trefor – and David!'

Dapple moved to greet Snowy, who ran in delight to his friend. Effans beamed. Trefor's blue eyes shone. Only David did not greet them eagerly. He kept his eyes on the ground and seemed ashamed.

'He got it hot and strong from Mrs Evans when he arrived back alone with the donkeys chasing after him,' explained Bill. 'I also had a few words to say to him, as you can imagine! So he now feels he can't look anyone in the face. It won't do him any harm to feel like that for a while. He behaved foolishly!'

'Poor David!' said Lucy-Ann. 'I expect he's sorry now,' and she spoke to the old man kindly. He looked at her gratefully.

'It's good to see you again, indeed to gootness it is, whateffer!' said Effans in his singing voice.

'Whateffer, whateffer!' shouted Kiki in delight. 'Look you, look you, whateffer!'

'That bird!' said Effans in great admiration. 'Look you, it iss a marvel, that bird. I would give ten pounds for a bird like that, whateffer!'

'She's not for sale,' said Jack, stroking Kiki. 'No, not for a million pounds. Where's the food, Effans? We're starving!'

'All explanations after the meal!' said Bill to Effans. 'We'll have a talk then, Effans, whilst the children go mad over the butterflies! Meier, Erlick, keep over there. Philip, tell the dogs to look after them.'

Effans stared in surprise at the two sullen men. Meier glared back. Erlick was full of self-pity, and had even begun to reproach Meier for his carelessness in letting them be captured. Meier looked at Erlick as if he could snap at him like the dogs.

'A pretty couple,' said Bill. 'I think we'll turn our backs on them. They spoil the view.'

Joyfully the children settled down to the finest picnic they had ever had. Mrs Evans had indeed surpassed herself. There was roast chicken, tender tongue, spiced ham, hard-boiled eggs, cucumbers, tomatoes, potted meat, fresh fruit, home-made lemonade which Effans had cleverly left cooling in a near-by stream, and so many other eatables that the boys despaired of even being able to taste them all!

They sat there on the hillside, the carpet of bright flowers spread at their feet – unbelievably brilliant in colour! And the butterflies!

'They're like flying flowers!' cried Lucy-Ann in joy. 'Hundreds of them! Thousands of them! What are they, Philip?'

'Fritillaries, painted ladies, commas, peacocks, ringlets, coppers, skippers, heaths . . .' reeled off Philip. 'My word, what a paradise of butterflies! I really will never forget this all my life long!'

It was a wonderful picnic – wonderful food, gorgeous butterflies, brilliant flowers – and plenty of laughter and jokes! Kiki was quite mad, and when she saw how Johns and Effans admired her, she showed off tremendously. She gave them her whole repertoire of noises, and Effans laughed till he choked.

The stolid Johns munched away, keeping his eyes on Kiki, and occasionally giving a slight smile at her more outrageous sayings.

'Indeed to gootness, whateffer! Wipe your feet and blow your nose. Pifflebunk! Pardon!'

Snowy wandered round, taking titbits from everyone. The dogs watched from a distance, feeling certain that their friend Philip would not forget them. It was a very good thing that Mrs Evans had provided so much, because with two prisoners and ten dogs every scrap of food would be needed!

Bill, Johns and Effans exchanged news when the children had gone to wander through the clouds of butterflies. Effans listened gravely. Trefor and David tried to understand, but most of what Bill said was beyond their English. Effans told them the story in Welsh later.

'They are brave children, look you,' said Effans. 'Very brave children, whateffer!'

30

The end of it all!

They had to sleep out in the open that night. Effans gave the children the rugs he had brought, because all their sleeping things had been left behind in the cave, on the mountain-side. The prisoners slept apart, guarded by the dogs. It was very warm, and Snowy got pushed off by everyone when he tried to cuddle down first on top of Philip, then on Jack, and then on the girls.

They had had a very long talk with Bill and told him all their adventures down to the last detail. Bill had marvelled at their accidental discovery of the strange mountain and its even stranger secret. He had examined the 'wings' which Philip had given to Johns to take care of for him.

'I shall take those back to school with me next term!' Philip said. 'Won't the boys stare! I bet some of them will want to try them!'

'Well, all I can say is I should discourage anyone from jumping off the school roof or anything like that, and trusting to these wings,' said Bill drily. 'I have a feeling that the ingenious brain behind these things is failing a little – the old "king" will never discover how to make the wings he so much wants to make. But he certainly has invented some remarkable things. I have had a talk with Meier, and he has told me why he believed in Monally – that's the "king's" real name.'

'Why did he believe in him?' asked the children curiously.

'Well, apparently he has, at one time or another, pro-duced the most remarkable inventions,' said Bill, 'and Meier has backed him and made a great deal of money out of them. How he came to find this mountain, and the rare metal in its heart, which the "king" wanted for his latest idea of conquering the pull of the earth, I haven't been able to find out yet. Some dirty work of some sort, I expect.'

'What are you going to do about everything?' asked Jack.

'Well – the paratroopers will be sent back home. The soldiers will be questioned and also sent back. I have a feeling there's something strange about them too. The "king" will be taken into safety,' said Bill. 'I shall send two or three scientists to the mountain to let them report on what they find there. I shouldn't be surprised if they advise us to destroy everything in it. The "king" has been meddling with dangerous things. With no one there to keep a guiding hand on them there might be a vast explosion.'

'It's a good thing we discovered it, isn't it?' said Lucy-Ann.

'A very good thing,' said Bill. 'And it's an even better thing you left that note with Dapple. If it hadn't been for that I'd never have found you.'

'What happened?' asked Jack.

'I came along to find you, complete with donkeys, after David's rush home,' said Bill. 'Instead I found only Dapple – and the note, which talked of very peculiar things indeed, and made me smell a very large rat.'

'Go on,' said Philip, interested.

'Well, I snooped round but couldn't find my way in through the roofless cave,' said Bill. 'So the only thing to do was to start finding out about helicopters. If somebody could land on that mountain-top, then so could I!'

'Good old Bill!' said Jack.

'And then,' said Bill, 'I found when I began making enquiries about all the helicopters in this country, who owned them and so on, that other people were also making enquiries about a few of them! Some of the helicopters had been flying off in suspicious circumstances, nobody knew where. So the police were even then enquiring into the matter – and I joined them, hotfoot!'

'And what did you find?' asked Dinah.

'I found a young pilot, with a terrific scar across his face!' said Bill. 'Ah – you know him, I see. And he spilt the beans, as we say! Told us he was worried about para-troopers jumping without proper parachutes and so on. And so, when he went on holiday, I took his place on the next helicopter trip – and hey presto, there I was on the top of the mountain!'

'Oh, Bill – it was heavenly to see you!' said Lucy-Ann.

Bill had told them all about Mrs Mannering too – how anxious she had been – how her hand had healed very well – and how she had begged in vain to be allowed to come with Effans and the others to meet the children, with the donkeys.

It was a long time before the children could go to sleep that night, for the day had been so exciting. The dogs lay and snoozed, one eye on the prisoners. The don-keys lay peacefully together. Snowy, sent off by each of the children, wandered off to Dapple and lay down beside him. Dapple was very pleased.

They got back to the farmhouse by dinner-time the next day, for Bill had got them all up very early the next morning. Mrs Mannering ran out in joy. She had been very worried indeed.

Mrs Evans followed. 'Indeed to gootness, it's grand to see you, whateffer! To think what you have been through, look you – as much danger as in war-time! It's glad we are to see you back!'

'It's well they are looking, too,' said Effans, in his up-and-down voice, beaming. 'And that bird, indeed, she is funnier than ever!'

'Whateffer, look you!' mimicked Kiki, also in a sing-song voice, and Effans went off into guffaws, imitated by Kiki. The two of them sounded so jolly that everyone else began to laugh too!

Mrs Evans, of course, had got another lovely meal ready for them all. And *what* a lot there were to feed that day too! She even found a fine supply of bones for the dogs, and Philip had to take them a good way off because Mrs Mannering said she really couldn't bear to hear such a munching and crunching as the ten dogs made short work of the bones.

What a lot there was to tell! Mrs Evans' eyes nearly fell out of her head as she listened, and handed out food of all kinds to everyone.

'To think of the children doing such things, look you!' she kept saying. 'Inside that mountain, indeed! Down in that pit too, look you!'

'Pardon, look you!' said Kiki, and gave a loud sneeze. Effans choked and Kiki copied him, making such a dreadful noise that Mrs Mannering said she was to go out of the room if she couldn't behave herself.

'Oh, Aunt Allie – she's just so glad she's back again,' said Jack, tapping Kiki on the beak.

'Send for the doctor,' said Kiki, fixing her wicked little eyes on Effans, who was still choking with laughter. 'Send for the weasel! Send for the look-you!'

Nobody could help laughing. Jack gave Kiki a very large plum, hoping to keep her quiet. Holding it in one clawed foot, Kiki dug her beak into it, making juice squirt all over poor Effans.

'Pardon!' said Kiki in delight, and did it again. Effans felt that he would exchange every one of his sheep for a bird like that. He watched Kiki and quite forgot to eat.

Johns was to take the prisoners down to the town, with David, escorted by two of the dogs. Mrs Evans said she would keep the rest of them at the farmhouse until the police had decided what to do with them.

'Mother – I suppose we couldn't possibly keep two or three of the dogs, could we?' asked Philip longingly.

'Good gracious, no!' said his mother. 'It's bad enough being landed with so many of your pets when you go back to school – but to have three great hungry Alsatians to look after would just kill me! No, they will be happier as police dogs.'

Bill was to stay until two or three scientists arrived to go with him to the mountain. Some police officers were to accompany them too, to round up the soldiers – though Bill did not expect any trouble from them at all. They probably had bad records, and had signed on with Meier to keep out of the way of the police for a while and to earn money.

'Can we go to the mountain too?' asked Jack hopefully. 'You might lose your way inside, Bill.'

'Oh, no I shan't,' said Bill. 'I found a nice little map of the inside of the mountain in Meier's pocket. I shan't lose my way – and you may as well give up all hope of coming with me, because you've been in quite enough danger these holidays. I'm afraid if I took you with me, another adventure might blow up – I never saw such children for smelling out adventures! I believe if I took you to visit my dear old aunt, we should find she had suddenly been kidnapped in a submarine, and you were forced to go to the other end of the world to rescue her!'

The boys were very disappointed not to go with Bill back to the mountain. Neither of the girls wanted to. Lucy-Ann was quite certain about that.

'I don't mind the adventure a bit, now it's all over and we can talk about it,' she said. 'But I didn't like it at the time. I hated that rumbling old mountain. Bill, Philip's going to let me wear his wings this afternoon in return for when I offered to jump from the helicopter instead of him. I shall fly from that high rock up there down to the farmhouse!'

'Indeed you won't!' said Bill promptly. Lucy-Ann laughed at Bill's shocked face.

'It's all right. I was only pulling your leg,' she said. 'But I'm going to wear them for a little while, and jump about, flapping them. Won't the hens be surprised?'

'Very,' said Bill. 'You'll stop them laying eggs, I should think! Look after her, Philip. See she doesn't do anything mad.'

Philip grinned. 'Lucy-Ann's all right,' he said. 'She's the most sensible one of us all.'

He put his hand into his pocket to feel if Sally the

slow-worm was there. An astonished expression came over his face. He gave a yell.

'Oh! Whatever's the matter!' said Lucy-Ann, jumping in fright.

'The most *wonder*ful thing has happened!' said Philip. 'Honestly, I never thought it of Sally.'

'What? What?' cried the others. Philip brought out his hand and opened it. It was full of what looked like little silvery darning needles, all wriggling about.

'Sally's babies! Mother, look! My slow-worm has got a whole lot of baby ones in my pocket. Oh, Mother, I don't believe any slow-worm has ever done that before to anyone! It's absolutely unique! Aren't they *lovely*?'

'Ugh!' said Dinah.

'Perfect!' said Jack.

'Do give me one for myself,' said Lucy-Ann. 'Oh, Philip! This is much, much more exciting than our adventure!'

'Much,' agreed Philip. 'Good old Sally! I've never had baby slow-worms for pets before – now I've got heaps.'

'You're not to keep them in your pocket, Philip,' said his mother. 'It's not good for them or for you.'

'But Sally will be so disappointed,' said Philip, in dismay.

The adventure was forgotten. All four heads bent over the silvery little creatures in Philip's palm. Snowy came to look. Kiki bent down from Jack's shoulders.

'Look you, whateffer!' she said, with her head on one

side, and opened her beak to hiccup. She caught Mrs Mannering's eye and changed her mind.

'Pardon!' she screeched and went off into a cackle of laughter. 'Bad Kiki! Send for the doctor, look you! Wipe your feet and blow your pardon!'

Don't miss . . .

The *Ship* of adventure

*the next exciting book in Enid Blyton's
thrilling Adventure series*

1

A grand holiday plan

'Mother's got something up her sleeve,' said Philip Mannering. 'I know she has. She's gone all mysterious.'

'Yes,' said his sister, Dinah. 'And whenever I ask what we're going to do these hols she just says "Wait and see!" As if we were about ten years old!'

'Where's Jack?' said Philip. 'We'll see if he knows what's up with Mother.'

'He's gone out with Lucy-Ann,' said Dinah. 'Ah – I can hear old Kiki screeching. They're coming!'

Jack and Lucy-Ann Trent came in together, looking very much alike with their red hair, green eyes and dozens of freckles. Jack grinned.

'Hallo! You ought to have been with us just now. A dog barked at Kiki, and she sat on a fence and mewed like a cat at him. You never saw such a surprised dog in your life!'

'He put his tail down and ran for his life,' said Lucy-Ann, scratching Kiki on the head. The parrot began to

3

mew again, knowing that the children were talking about her. Then she hissed and spat like an angry cat. The children laughed.

'If you'd done that to the dog he'd have died of astonishment,' said Jack. 'Good old Kiki. Nobody can be dull when you're about.'

Kiki began to sway herself from side to side, and made a crooning noise. Then she went off into one of her tremendous cackles.

'Now you're showing off,' said Philip. 'Don't let's take any notice of her. She'll get noisy and Mother will come rushing in.'

'That reminds me – what's Mother gone all mysterious about?' said Dinah. 'Lucy-Ann, haven't you noticed it?'

'Well – Aunt Alison *does* act rather as if she's got something up her sleeve,' said Lucy-Ann, considering the matter. 'Rather like she does before somebody's birthday. *I* think she's got a plan for the summer holidays.'

Jack groaned. 'Blow! I've got a perfectly good plan too. Simply wizard. I'd better get mine in before Aunt Allie gets hers.'

'What's yours?' asked Dinah, with interest. Jack always had wonderful plans, though not many of them came to anything.

'Well – I thought we could all go off together on our

bikes, taking a tent with us – and camp out in a different place each night,' said Jack. 'It would be super.'

The others looked at him scornfully. 'You suggested that *last* hols and the hols before,' said Dinah. 'Mother said "No" then, and she's not likely to say "Yes" now. It *is* a good plan, going off absolutely on our own like that – but ever since we've had so many adventures Mother simply won't hear of it.'

'Couldn't your mother come with us?' suggested Lucy-Ann hopefully.

'Now *you're* being silly,' said Dinah. 'Mother's a dear – but grown-ups are so frightfully particular about things. We'd have to put our macs on at the first spot of rain, and coats if the sun went in, and I wouldn't be surprised if we didn't each have to have an umbrella strapped to our bike-handles.'

The others laughed. 'I suppose it *wouldn't* do to ask Aunt Allie too, then,' said Lucy-Ann. 'What a pity!'

'What a pity, what a pity,' agreed Kiki at once. 'Wipe your feet and shut the door, where's your hanky, naughty boy!'

'Kiki's got the idea, all right!' said Philip. 'That's the kind of thing that even the nicest grown-ups say, isn't it, Kiki, old bird?'

'Bill isn't like that,' said Lucy-Ann at once. 'Bill's fine.'

Everyone agreed at once. Bill Cunningham, or Bill Smugs as he had first called himself to them, was their very firm friend, and had shared all their adventures with them. Sometimes they had dragged him into them, and sometimes it was the other way round – he had got into one and they had followed. It really did seem, sometimes, as Mrs Mannering said, that adventures cropped up wherever Bill and the children were.

'*I* had an idea for these hols too,' said Philip. 'I thought it would be pretty good fun to camp down by the river, and look for otters. I've never had an otter for a pet. Lovely things they are. I thought—'

'You *would* think of a thing like that,' said Dinah, half crossly. 'Just because you're mad on all kinds of creatures from fleas to – to . . .'

'Elephants,' said Jack obligingly.

'From fleas to elephants, you think everyone else is,' said Dinah. 'What a frightful holiday – looking for wet, slimy otters – and having them in the tent at night, I suppose – and all kinds of other horrible things too.'

'Shut up, Dinah,' said Philip. 'Otters aren't horrible. They're lovely. You should just see them swimming under the water. And by the way, I'm *not* mad on fleas. *Or* mosquitoes. *Or* horse-flies. I think they're interesting, but you can't say I've ever had things like that for pets.'

'What about those earwigs you had once – that escaped out of the silly cage you made for them? Ugh! And that stag beetle that did tricks? And that—'

'Oh, gosh! Now we're off!' said Jack, seeing one of the familiar quarrels breaking out between Philip and hot-headed Dinah. 'I suppose we're going to listen to a long list of Philip's pets now! Anyway, here comes Aunt Allie. We can ask her what she thinks of our holiday ideas. Get yours in first, Philip.'

Mrs Mannering came in, with a booklet in her hand. She smiled round at the four children, and Kiki put up her crest in delighted welcome.

'Wipe your feet and shut the door,' she said, in a friendly tone. 'One, two, three, GO!' She made a noise like a pistol shot after the word 'go', and Mrs Mannering jumped in fright.

'It's all right, Mother – she keeps doing that ever since she came to our school sports, and heard the starter yelling to us, and letting off his pistol,' grinned Philip. 'Once she made the pistol-shot noise just when we were all in a line, ready to start – and off we went long before time! You should have heard her cackle. Bad bird!'

'Naughty Polly, poor Polly, what a pity, what a pity,' said Kiki. Jack tapped her on the beak.

'Be quiet. Parrots should be seen and not heard. Aunt Allie, we've just been talking about holiday plans. I thought it would be a super idea if you'd let us all go off on our bikes – ride where we liked and camp out each night. I know you've said we couldn't when I asked you before, but—'

'I say "No" again,' said Mrs Mannering very firmly.

'Well, Mother, could we go off to the river and camp there, because I want to find out more about the otters?'

said Philip, not taking any notice of Dinah's scowl. 'You see—'

'*No*, Philip,' said his mother, just as firmly as before. 'And you know why I won't let you go on expeditions like that. I should have thought you would have given up asking me by now.'

'But *why* won't you let us go?' wailed Lucy-Ann. 'We shall be quite safe.'

'Now, Lucy-Ann, you know perfectly well that as soon as I let you four out of my sight when holidays come, you *immediately* – yes, *immediately* – fall into the most frightful adventures imaginable.' Mrs Mannering sounded quite fierce. 'And I am quite determined that these holidays you are not going off *any*where on your own, so it's just no good your asking me.'

'But, Mother, that's just silly,' said Philip in dismay. 'You speak as if we go out *looking* for adventures. We don't. And I ask you – what possible adventure could we fall into if we just went down to the river to camp? Why, you could come and see us for yourself every evening if you wanted to.'

'Yes – and the very first evening I came I should find you all spirited away somewhere, and mixed up with robbers and spies or rogues of some kind,' said his mother. 'Think of some of your holidays – first you get lost down an old copper mine on a deserted island, then another time you get shut up in the dungeons of an old castle, mixed up with spies—'

'Oooh yes – and another time we got into the wrong aeroplane and were whisked off to the Valley of Adventure,' said Lucy-Ann, remembering. 'That was when we found all those amazing stolen statues hidden in caves – how their eyes gleamed when we saw them! I thought they were alive, but they weren't.'

'And the next time we went off with Bill to the bird-islands,' said Jack. 'That was grand. We had two tame puffins – do you remember, Philip?'

'Huffin and Puffin,' put in Kiki at once.

'Quite right, old bird,' said Philip. 'Huffin and Puffin they were. I loved them.'

'You may have gone to look for birds – but you found a whole nest of rogues,' said his mother. 'Gun-runners! Terribly dangerous.'

'Well, Mother, what about last summer hols?' said Dinah. '*You* nearly got caught up in *that* adventure!'

'Horrible!' said Mrs Mannering with a shiver. 'That awful mountain with its weird secrets – and the mad King of the Mountain – you nearly didn't escape from there. No – I tell you quite definitely that you can never again go off anywhere by yourselves. I'm always coming with you!'

There was a silence at this. All four children were very fond of Mrs Mannering – but they did like being on their own for some part of each holiday.

'Well – Aunt Allie – suppose Bill came with us – wouldn't that be all right?' asked Lucy-Ann. 'I do always feel safe with Bill.'

'Bill can't be trusted to keep out of adventures either,' said Mrs Mannering. 'He's grand, I know, and I'd trust him more than anyone else in the world. But when you and he get together there's just no knowing what will happen. So, these holidays, I've made a very safe plan – and dear old Bill isn't in it, so perhaps we shall keep away from danger and extraordinary happenings.'

'What's your plan, Mother?' said Dinah nervously. '*Don't* say we're going to a seaside hotel or anything like that. They'd never take Kiki.'

'I'm taking you all for a cruise on a big ship,' said Mrs Mannering, and she smiled. 'I know you'll like that. It's tremendous fun. We shall call at all sorts of places, and see all kinds of strange and exciting things. And I shall have you under my eye, in one place all the time – the ship will be our home for some time, and if we get off at various ports we shall all go in a party together. There won't be a chance of any strange adventure.'

The four children looked at one another. Kiki watched them. Philip spoke first.

'It does sound rather exciting, Mother! Yes, it really does. We've never been on a really big ship before. Of course, I shall miss having any *animals* . . .'

'Oh, Philip – surely you can go without your ever-lasting menagerie of creatures!' cried Dinah. 'I must say it'll be a great relief to *me* to know you haven't got mice somewhere about you, or lizards, or slow-worms!

10

Mother, it sounds super, I think. Thanks awfully for thinking up something so exciting.'

'Yes – it sounds smashing,' said Jack. 'We'll see no end of birds I've never seen before.'

'Jack's happy so long as he's somewhere that will provide him with birds,' said Lucy-Ann with a laugh. 'What with Philip with his craze for all kinds of creatures, and Jack with his passion for birds, it's a good thing we two girls haven't got crazes for anything as well. Aunt Allie, it's a wizard plan of yours. When do we go?'

'Next week,' said Mrs Mannering. 'That will give us plenty of time to get our things ready and packed. It will be very warm on the cruise, so we must get plenty of thin clothes to wear. White's the best thing – it doesn't hold the heat so much. And you must all have sun-hats the whole time, so don't begin to moan about wearing hats.'

'Isn't Bill coming?' asked Philip.

'No,' said his mother firmly. 'I feel rather mean about it, because he's just finished the job he's on, and he wants a holiday. But this time he's *not* coming with us. I want a nice peaceful holiday with no adventure at all.'

'Poor Bill,' said Lucy-Ann. 'Still – I daresay he'll be glad to have a holiday without us, for a change. I say – it's going to be fun, isn't it?'

'Fun!' said Kiki, joining in, and letting off a screech of excitement. 'Fun, fun, fun!'

The  of adventure

Something very sinister is happening on the mysterious Isle of Gloom and the children are determined to uncover the truth!

But Philip, Dinah, Lucy-Ann and Jack are not prepared for the dangerous adventure that awaits them in the abandoned copper mines and secret tunnels beneath the sea.

The  of adventure

Why is everyone so afraid of the castle on the hill, and what dark secrets lurk inside its walls?

When flashing lights are seen in a distant tower, Philip, Dinah, Lucy-Ann and Jack decide to investigate – and discover a very sinister plot concealed within its hidden rooms and gloomy underground passages.

The

Who are the two strange pilots, and what is the secret treasure hidden in the lonely valley where the children land?

Nothing could be more exciting than a daring night flight on Bill's plane! But Philip, Dinah, Lucy-Ann and Jack soon find themselves flying straight into a truly amazing adventure.

The *Sea* of adventure

A mysterious trip to the desolate Northern Isles soon turns
into a terrifying adventure when Bill is kidnapped!

Marooned far from the mainland on a deserted coast,
Philip, Dinah, Lucy-Ann and Jack find themselves playing a
dangerous game with an unknown enemy. Will they escape
with Bill and their lives?

The *Mountain*
of adventure

Surely a peaceful holiday in the Welsh mountains will keep
the children out of trouble! But the mystery of a rumbling
mountain soon has them thirsty for more adventure.

Philip, Dinah, Lucy-Ann and Jack are determined to explore
the mountain and uncover its secret, but first they must
escape from a pack of ravenous wolves and a mad genius
who plans to rule the world!

The **Ship**

of adventure

An amazing voyage around the beautiful Greek islands becomes an exciting quest to find the lost treasure of the Andra!

Philip, Dinah, Lucy-Ann and Jack are plunged into a search for hidden riches – with some ruthless villains hot on their trail! Will they find the treasure before it's too late?

The *Circus*

of adventure

Why did Bill have to bring the babyish Gustavus with them on holiday? Jack knows he'll only be trouble . . .

But when Gustavus is kidnapped, along with Philip, Dinah and Lucy-Ann, Jack bravely sets out to rescue them, leading him to a faraway land and the discovery of a plot to kill the King!

The *River* of adventure

A river cruise through ancient desert lands becomes a mysterious adventure when Bill disappears!

While Philip, Dinah, Lucy-Ann and Jack are desperately searching for Bill, they become trapped beneath a forgotten temple where no one has set foot for 7,000 years. What dangers lurk within, and will they ever escape?